Legacy of Love

By

Linda Shenton

Matchett

Legacy of Love
By Linda Shenton Matchett

Cover Design and author photo by: V. McKevitt

PHOTO CREDITS:

ISBN-13: 978-1-7347085-8-5

Published by Shortwave Press

This is a work of fiction. Names, characters, places, and incidents either are the products of the author's imagination or are used fictitiously. Any resemblance to actual events or persons, living or dead, is entirely coincidental

Chapter One

Voices mingled with the clink of silverware on china, as Meg Underwood threaded her way between the tables at the Staghead Café toward the handsome stranger seated near the door. In the dozen years since Oregon had achieved statehood, settlers continued to flock to America's great Northwest, but the tiny town didn't see many of them. Those who did arrive usually had a story to tell, herself included.

She patted her hair and smoothed her frilly, white apron as she approached him. His background was none of her business, although if he stayed any length of time, the rumor mill would churn out bits and pieces. She pinned on a smile and dipped her head in greeting. "What can I get you?"

"How's the coffee here?"

"Excellent, if I do say so myself. And there's fresh apple pie if you have a hankering for something sweet."

His gaze raked her from head to toe. "I do, but not for my stomach."

Her eyebrow shot up, and she stiffened her spine. Apparently, the man's expensive, hand-tailored clothing made him think she'd be flattered by his innuendo. She was anything but. Having left wealth and the vacuous machinations of Boston society, she knew exactly the type of man he was, and she was definitely not interested. "Coffee, it is." She pivoted toward the kitchen.

"Hey, I'm not finished making my order, girlie." His voice held a combination of steel and condescension.

With a sigh, Meg turned back. "I think someone else may be better prepared to serve you, sir."

"But you're the one I want." The man grabbed her arm and yanked her toward him.

She stumbled and pitched forward, falling into the man's lap. He leered at her, his hot breath on her cheek a fetid combination of onions and cigar tobacco. She struggled to extricate herself. "Sir, please release me this instant."

"I heard Spruce Hill was a friendly town. Guess that's not the case." His lips twisted into a frown.

Heavy footsteps sounded behind her, then firm hands pulled her upright. "We're right friendly until someone comes into town and accosts one of us. We don't take kindly to that sort of behavior."

Meg blew out a shuddering breath and scooted behind the towering form of Sheriff Hobbs then peeked over his shoulder at the visitor. *Thank You, God.*

"This is between me and the girl. Why don't you butt out?"

Sheriff Hobbs pulled aside his vest revealing the tin star on his shirt and the gun holstered at his waist. "Did I forget to mention I'm the sheriff of this fine town?"

The man paled, and his eyes widened. He bolted upright, crossing his arms. "No need to get the law involved. I was just kidding with her. It's not my fault she can't take a joke."

"You'll treat her with respect, and I won't have to throw you out." Sheriff Hobbs's voice was flinty, and Meg had no doubt his blue eyes sparked with fire.

"No, sir." The man tugged at his ear and glanced at Meg. "My apologies if I offended you, miss. It won't happen again. I'll just have some coffee and be on my way."

"All right." She squeezed the sheriff's arm as thanks for his rescue and made her way to the kitchen, her mind racing. If she wasn't mistaken, the stranger's accent was East Coast, not as far north as Boston, but close enough. She shivered. How much farther would she have to travel to avoid her past?

Her hand shook as she poured the coffee. Sloshing over the side of the chunky mug, the hot liquid scalded her fingers. She gasped and set down the cup with a bang. Tears sprang to her eyes. Foolish girl. He was not Tyler Armory, her rich, lecherous ex-fiancé, and he couldn't hurt her. The sheriff's intervention had ensured her safety.

"You okay, Meg?" Mrs. Krause, the restaurant's owner, as well as breakfast and lunch cook, peered at her with a concerned expression.

"Yes. I burned myself pouring the coffee."

Mrs. Krause tilted her head. "You seem a bit more agitated than just making a spill."

"It's nothing. One of the customers was...uh...a little too friendly, and it shook me up. I'm fine."

"Do I need to talk some sense into him?" She waved her long wooden spoon, a menacing glare darkening her face.

Meg giggled at the woman's offer. Even though she barely stood more than five feet tall, Helga Krause had put the fear of God in more than a few ornery customers. Widowed after her husband brought her to America from Germany during the gold rush of sixty-two then died in a claim dispute, she'd traveled to the coast and settled in Spruce Hill. The town loved her bratwurst, cucumber-potato salad, and *baumkuchen*, the slices of which resembled tree rings, but Meg's favorite was *lebkuchen*, the traditional Christmas cookies of Mrs. Krause's home country. "Thanks, but Sheriff Hobbs took care of the situation."

"A good man. I'll be sure to ladle him an extra helping of stew next time he's in."

"I'd appreciate that." The sheriff poked his head through the door and smiled. He reached for the mug and winked at Meg. "Think I'll give our *guest* his beverage and save you a trip."

"Thanks, Sheriff. I owe you one."

"Nonsense. I enjoy making these young'uns squirm, and he seemed to need a comeuppance more than most. Glad to help." He disappeared, and his footsteps faded.

Mrs. Krause jerked her head toward a chair near the back door. "Sit down and take a break. The lunch rush is over, so I'll keep an eye on the dining room while you rest."

"Are you sure?"

"Absolutely." She pointed to a newspaper peeking out from the satchel hanging on a hook. "Didn't you tell me you're from Boston? Mr. Densley had an old edition of the *Boston Herald* no one claimed, so he let me borrow it. Why don't you catch up on the news from home?"

Meg's heart pounded. Did she want to know what was happening in her hometown? Five years had passed since her departure in the dead of night. Surely there wouldn't be any news of interest to her. She shrugged and retrieved the paper then dropped onto the seat. Perhaps reading the periodical would validate her decision to leave.

She unfolded the paper and scanned the headlines. Near the bottom of the first page, her gaze riveted on the boldface print: "SOCIAL ACTIVIST AND PHILANTHROPIST IDA NORTHCOTT DEAD AT 75."

Her eyes welled, and her lower lip trembled. Aunt Ida. The woman who'd supported her decision to flee Boston and had, in fact, purchased Meg's train ticket. When she left, she'd hoped to see her mother's sister again, but the years had trickled past, and Meg's fear had rooted her feet on the West Coast.

Now, she'd never have a chance to embrace her auntie again. To tell her about the wonderful people of Spruce Hill, who'd accepted Meg as one of their own. A condolence letter to Mother was out of the question. None of her family must ever find out where she lived.

Chapter Two

Sunlight streamed through the window and glared into Reuben Jessop's eyes as he stood at attention in front of his boss, Allan Pinkerton. Founder of the agency that bore his name, he was a medium-built man, but the steely gaze set deep in his fully bearded face commanded the respect of operatives and criminals alike.

Reuben swallowed. Would he be found guilty of negligence in the death of his partner?

"Stand down, Jessop." Pinkerton's Scottish brogue lent a musical cadence to his speech. "You look as if you're facing a firing squad."

"Yes, sir." The man wasn't far off. Being summoned to the famous detective's office, Reuben felt kinship to condemned prisoners.

"I apologize for taking so long to investigate the circumstances surrounding Eddie's demise. He was a good man and an outstanding operative. The two of you made a first-rate team. His loss will reverberate through the ranks, and I know you feel his death personally."

A nod was all Reuben could manage. He and Eddie Watkins had been more like brothers than partners. Seemingly able to read each other's thoughts, they'd been watching each other's backs since the early days of the war when they were assigned to the 1st Cavalry Division. Chancellorsville had been a nightmare, but they'd survived that battle and more until being transferred to Lincoln's personal guard.

"After much consideration, I don't believe you could or should have responded differently to the events as they played out. You are completely absolved of any wrongdoing or mistakes. Eddie's death was a tragedy, but I'm not convinced it was preventable." Pinkerton stroked his beard. "But he did not die in vain. You can rest in the fact that you were able to apprehend a dangerous group of men we've been pursuing for months. Well done, Jessop."

"Thank you, sir." Tension seeped from Reuben's shoulders. Good to know he wouldn't lose his job, but working with another operative held no allure. Maybe it was time to quit and move on to a new career. He shook his head. Being a lawman was the only job he knew how to do. "Will that be all, sir?"

"No. I've got another case if you're interested. I won't force you to take it because the search is a personal favor for a friend. I'd handle it myself, but unfortunately, I'm too well known."

One of America's success stories, Pinkerton had emigrated to America almost twenty years ago and entered the police force shortly thereafter. While working in intelligence during the war he thwarted an alleged assassination attempt on Lincoln. His boss was tenacious and since then had ensured the arrest of numerous gang members and train robbers, but his achievements came at the cost of anonymity.

"I'm to be undercover, then?" Reuben's heart sped up, and he smiled. His favorite type of work as an operative was to infiltrate a group to conduct the investigation.

"No, but the situation requires a certain...delicacy."

"I'm not exactly a ballroom-and-parlor kind of guy, sir."

Pinkerton chuckled and shook his head. "Not that kind of delicacy, son, although kid gloves might be required."

"You've got me intrigued, Mr. Pinkerton. I won't let you down."

"But I haven't given you the job specifications yet. Are you sure you want to take the case?"

"If you think I'm the best agent, who am I to question your wisdom?"

"You're a good man, Jessop. The assignment is an easy one, and you should be home by Christmas if not sooner. I need you to go to Oregon and escort a young woman to Boston who is Ida Northcott's niece and heir."

"As a bodyguard?"

"No, safety isn't the issue, but the family attorney isn't convinced she'll return without a personal invitation, as it were."

Reuben's stomach hollowed. Any junior agent could handle attendant responsibilities. Was the case really a favor for a friend, or did Mr. Pinkerton not trust him to handle a serious mission? Would he have to prove himself all over again?

Pinkerton rose and walked around the desk until he stood next to Reuben. "You think I'm punishing you—"

"No, sir—"

"I understand your concerns. At the surface, this assignment seems like a waste of time for a senior operative. But there is a certain delicacy required as the young woman in question belongs to a fairly well-placed family within Boston society. The utmost care must be taken to ensure the situation remains out of the public eye. Is that clear?"

"Absolutely."

"Excellent." Pinkerton leaned over the desk and opened a folder then picked up a small photograph that he handed to Reuben. "This is Meg Underwood, who is a waitress at the Staghead Café in Spruce Hill, Oregon. She may require a bit of...uh...persuasion to return with you to Boston. See Miss Gibson on your way out. In anticipation of your acceptance of the case, I had her prepare your mission files and secure your funds." He squeezed Reuben's shoulder. "Best of luck, son."

"Thank you, sir." Reuben pivoted on his heel and strode from the office. He glanced at the woman's photograph and nearly stumbled. Dark hair coiffed around a heart-shaped face, she was beautiful. Her fair skin appeared porcelainlike. A demure smile clung to her lips, but piercing dark eyes set wide above her cheekbones were her most striking feature. This girl was no shrinking violet. He'd have his work cut out for him.

Why would a wealthy young woman flee one of Boston's elite families? He had secrets. Apparently, she did too.

Chapter Three

A light breeze wafted the briny sea air into the café through the open windows. Balancing several plates on her arm, Meg approached the table where a quartet of elderly women chattered and giggled like schoolgirls. "All right, ladies, I've got your orders right here." She deftly distributed the dishes and smiled. "Will that be all?"

"Yes, thank you." One of the women who had snow-white hair piled high on her head inhaled deeply. "This smells heavenly, dear. Tell Mrs. Krause she's outdone herself today."

"Yes, ma'am. She is a wonderful cook." Meg circulated through the tables checking on the other diners.

Minnie Hobbs, who arrived almost a year ago before Christmas to become the town's new schoolteacher and found love with the sheriff's son, sat with Amy Powell, wife of the local cannery owner. The two were closer than barnacles on a ship, and their heads were bent together as she neared. "How are you gals today? Looks like you're plotting something."

They looked up and grinned, and Amy wiggled her eyebrows. "Maybe. We were talking about whose turn it is to get married, and we had just come to your name on the list."

"You've made a list?" Meg shook her head. "Surely, you have better things to do than act as the town matchmakers."

Minnie shrugged. "We think everyone should be as happy as we are, and you must be lonely, so it only stands that we should try to help you remedy the situation."

Meg rolled her eyes. "I'm quite content. I've got a job I enjoy, a nice place to live, and good friends. Even if they are a couple of busybodies."

"Contentment is not the same as being happy." Minnie pushed a potato chunk around her plate. "You're a sweet girl. You deserve to find love, and we aim to help you."

"No, thank you. I'll let you know if I need any help finding a husband, but I'm not in the market." Meg put her hands on her hips. "Now, can I bring you anything else?"

"Give us a few more minutes, then we'll have some of Mrs. Krause's fabulous apple strudel." Amy sighed. "I'm nearly stuffed, but I hate to leave without any."

"How about if I wrap it up for you?"

"That would be lovely." She winked at Meg. "See? You're so thoughtful. A girl like you deserves a husband who will dote on her."

"Enough." Face warm, Meg shook her finger at the young women. "Pick on someone else." She whirled and stopped at another table, Amy's chuckles following her. "Good afternoon, Nadina. Are you enjoying your meal?"

A member of the church, Nadina grinned and laid her knife and fork on her empty plate then wiped her mouth with a napkin. "You know they're never going to give up. That pair is relentless."

"They mean well." Meg picked up the soiled dinnerware. "But I really am satisfied with my life here in Spruce Hill."

"I thought I was too, then I met Michael. You'll know when you meet the man of your dreams."

"Well, he'd better come from out of town, because all the good prospects are already taken." Meg tilted her head. "You might have gotten the last of them."

"Have you thought of being a mail-order bride?"

"No. Remember I'm not looking for love." She laughed. "You're as bad as Amy and Minnie. I'll bring your bill."

"Don't discount the possibilities." Nadina pressed coins into Meg's hand. "I've got to run, but that should cover my charges."

"See you soon." Meg surveyed the remaining tables. Everyone had been checked on, so she ducked into the kitchen to wrap dessert for the pair of coconspirators. A grin tugged at her lips. Today was not the first time they'd indicated she should try her hand at love. "According to one of our guests you've outdone yourself, Mrs. Krause."

The cook beamed, her face flushed and damp with sweat. "*Danke.* And how are you holding up? Lots more diners than usual."

"My feet are starting to complain, but everyone is set for now, so I was going to sit for a few minutes unless you need my help."

"*Nein.* You rest."

"Are you sure?" Meg searched the woman's face. She only peppered her speech with German when she was tired or upset. She'd been at the stove for hours. She deserved a break more than Meg.

"*Ja.* As you said, we're caught up with orders. I'll watch the dining room."

"All right." Meg went out the back door, and the wind cooled her face. It might be November outside, but the kitchen felt like Boston in August.

She scrubbed at her face with cold fingers. What would she be doing at this moment if she'd stayed and followed through with her parents' plans for her to marry Tyler? Certainly not waiting tables. More likely being waited on herself.

His face sprang to mind. Handsome in an aristocratic way with a high forehead and patrician nose, he had gray eyes that scrutinized his surroundings with arrogance and disdain. During their few conversations, he'd barely let her speak then belittled all of her opinions. She shuddered. She'd definitely made the right decision when she fled. A life with a man like Tyler would be miserable.

Her parents' marriage wasn't perfect, but they loved each other. Chest tightening, she rubbed the back of her neck. Despite their desire to improve their standing in the community by selling her off in marriage, they loved her. They were probably worried about her, but she couldn't set their mind at ease with a letter. Even after five years, she didn't trust them not to send someone to retrieve her.

What about a mail-order marriage? Was Amy's idea a good one? No. Mail-order brides traveled inland to the plains. Being in the middle of nowhere as a farmwife was not a lifestyle Meg could adhere to. She loved living on the coast and in Spruce Hill.

"Meg? We've got a new customer."

"Coming." Meg went back inside, grabbed the coffeepot and a mug, and walked through the kitchen into the dining hall. Her gaze swept the tables and came to rest on one with a lone diner. He raised his head and met her eyes, his ice-blue stare traveling from her face to her feet. Deeply tanned, his face was handsome in a rugged sort of way, his jaw square and jutted forward. High cheekbones gave him an angular appearance. Jet-black hair was combed back, worn slightly longer than most visitors from the East. And he was definitely from the East. Of that she was certain.

She licked her lips then forced a smile as she strode toward his table. "Coffee?"

"Sure." He leaned back in his chair and laced his fingers. "You must know a lot of the townspeople. Can you tell me where I might find Meg Underwood?"

She froze, and her mouth dried. How did this man find her and who was he?

***

Having memorized Miss Underwood's photograph during the trek from Chicago to Oregon, Reuben knew the beautiful waitress who gaped at him was the young woman he sought. He'd pored over the file he'd received from the agency's secretary, gleaning every scrap of information about his target and her family. Even though she wore a simple white blouse and black skirt covered with a starched, white apron, she looked every inch the heiress she was.

Spine straight and shoulders thrown back, she appeared taller than her five feet five inches indicated in the folder. She looked down her nose at him, intelligence and wariness warring for supremacy in her walnut-brown eyes. Her skin was even more soft looking than in her picture. Her brown hair was shot through with highlights of red and cinnamon, and several strands had come loose from the bun at the base of her neck. He stifled the desire to tuck the tresses behind her small ears.

He'd spent much of the trip cogitating over the best approach to take with the woman and finally decided to feign ignorance of her identity upon meeting her. If his Pinkerton senses were correct, she was suspicious of him and his inquiry. He widened his eyes in hopes of adding an air of innocence to his features.

The waitress's eyes narrowed. "What business do you have with Miss Underwood?"

"I'd say that's personal, wouldn't you?"

Her face pinked, and she shrugged. "We tend to protect our own, and you're not from around here."

"Granted." He smiled. "Perhaps I should have introduced myself before blurting out my question. My name is Reuben Jessop, and I'm with the Pinkerton Detective Agency, with a matter of great important to Miss Underwood." He reached into his jacket pocket and pulled out a leather wallet from which he withdrew a small card that he displayed for her.

Her gaze flicked from the card to his face, and her shoulders slumped as she sent him a curt nod.

He put away his identification card. Best to proceed slowly or she might bolt. "How about some of that coffee, now?"

"Of course." She poured the steaming dark brew into the mug and seemed to watch him from the corner of her eye. Her hand shook, and the coffee spilled over the side of the cup and into his lap.

The hot liquid seeped through his blue jeans, and he leapt to his feet with a shout. He pulled the wet fabric away from his legs and glared at her. Had she doused him on purpose?

"Oh! I'm terribly sorry. How clumsy of me." She pulled a towel from the pocket of her apron and reached toward the spreading stain on his pants then froze and dropped the cloth. "Are you hurt? Should you see the doctor?" Her face was deep red to the roots of her hair.

He blew out a sigh. The sopping fabric had cooled. "No, I'm none the worse for wear."

"You must let me launder your clothes." Her eyes were moist, and her lower lip trembled. "It's the least I can do."

"There's no need. This isn't the first time I've been a mess." He winked at her. "Nor will it be the last." He laid his hand on her arm. "It's my own fault for upsetting you, Miss Underwood."

She gaped at him. "Why did you pretend not to know me? Why are you here? What do you want?"

Reuben tugged at his collar. "I thought it would be better this way. Apparently, I was wrong. Anyway, I've come to take you back to Boston with me. Your Aunt Ida has passed away and left you her estate." Conversation in the room ceased, and Reuben cringed. A sidelong glance around the room told him that every ear in the room was tuned in to their exchange. So much for handling things with kid gloves.

"How dare you blurt out my business in public, Mr. Jessop." Her mouth was set in a slash, and her eyes sparked with anger. "I think it's best if you leave. Go back to wherever you're staying for your coffee."

She whirled, stomped to the kitchen, and disappeared from sight.

He needed to fix this. And fast. He shoved his chair and hurried to the kitchen where he poked his head over the swinging doors. "Miss Underwood?"

An elderly woman glared at him from the stove, but Miss Underwood was nowhere in sight. "No customers allowed in the kitchen, especially those who make my Meg afraid."

"Afraid? I'm not here to hurt her. I have good news."

"*Ja*. She tells me her news, but she's not interested in money. You should give it to someone else."

"You don't understand. I have nothing to do with the bequest. I'm only here to escort her back to Boston to claim the funds."

"Meg is happy in Spruce Hill without wealth. I know all about her family, and she doesn't want the chains of having lots of money to bind her. To change who she is."

"But—"

"No more arguing. You need to leave and stay away from Meg."

"I will leave, and please tell her I'm sorry for how badly I handled...well...everything. I didn't mean to embarrass her, but I need to meet with her to give her a letter from her aunt's lawyer. I'll be in touch."

The woman continued to glower at him, and he ducked his head. She would give Allan Pinkerton a run for his money. He hurried to the table he'd vacated trying to ignore the stares of the remaining diners. Grabbing his hat, he plunked it on his head, and dashed out the door. He'd blown it. Big time. He had his work cut out for him to complete his mission to convince her to return East with him.

Mr. Pinkerton figured Reuben would have things tied up by Thanksgiving. He'd be lucky if he could get her out of Oregon by the time festivities for Independence Day rolled around.

Legacy of Love

Chapter Four

A knock sounded on the door of Meg's room, and a muffled voice said, "Meg, you've got a gentleman caller. Better hurry. He's a looker."

"Okay, thanks." Heart pounding in her chest, Meg stuffed a slip of paper between the pages of *Little Women*. Her first day off in a week, she'd hoped to spend the morning lounging and reading her favorite novel, but apparently Reuben Jessop was going to ruin today, too. She'd lay a week's wages on it. Finding out where her boarding house was wouldn't take much effort, and he seemed a tenacious sort of man.

What was his story? A handsome man who walked with the fluid grace and strength of a panther and spoke in a well-modulated voice surely had better job opportunities than one that required him to trek across the continent as a messenger boy. He'd dressed like a local, but his leather jacket fit as if hand-tailored, and his boots indicated money as well.

She'd heard of the Pinkerton agency from the newspaper and customers over the years, how its detectives often went undercover to get the job done. Was Mr. Jessop adorned in expensive clothing as part of the job because of her society upbringing or was he a dandy like Tyler?

Meg shook her head. No. He was definitely not like her ex-fiancé. That was obvious despite only spending a few tortuous minutes with the man. His piercing gaze was clear and his expression without guile. Tyler's, on the other hand, was typically clouded and shifty.

"Stop stalling, girl. Best get this thing over with." She grabbed her keys and tucked them in her skirt pocket then left her room without a backward glance. The boarding house was quiet. Being midweek, most of the other girls had probably gone to their jobs. She patted her hair and descended the stairs to the parlor where the residents were allowed to entertain male callers.

The rug in the hallway muffled her footsteps, but Mr. Jessop stood near the doorway, alert and waiting. And looking every bit as handsome as he did yesterday. Exceptional hearing must be a requirement of the job. "Good morning. Did you change your mind about allowing me to launder your clothing?"

"No." He smiled, and his eyes crinkled at the corners. Embarrassment played over his face. "I came to apologize for what happened at the café. My conduct was unprofessional and put you in a tenuous position. A junior operative would have handled the first meeting better than I did." His long, tapered fingers tightened on the black Stetson. "Please forgive me and allow me to begin anew."

Tongue-tied, she nodded. What was wrong with her? She was reacting like a schoolgirl.

"May I sit down?"

"Yes. Of course. Excuse my manners." She gestured to the upholstered Queen Anne chairs clustered around the fireplace. "I'm surprised to see you."

He reddened as they made their way to the furniture. "Another mistake. I shouldn't have come unannounced."

"Nonsense. Spruce Hill doesn't require calling cards or appointments." Legs trembling, she lowered herself on the nearest chair. Why did he have to be so good looking? Did the agency send him with the idea that his appearance would make her swoon and agree to the terms of the will? She pressed her lips together and laced her fingers. Well, they could forget about that tactic.

Sitting across from her, he continued to hold his hat as he leaned his arms on his thighs. "Thank you for seeing me. I wanted to give you the letter from the attorney and explain the situation." He reached into his jacket pocket, pulled out an envelope, and handed it to her.

Meg ran her fingernail under the flap and withdrew a single sheet of heavy ivory-colored paper, the top of which featured an embossed name and address. She scanned the words, and her breath hitched. A fresh wave of grief swept over her. She closed her eyes for a brief moment then folded the missive and slid it back into the envelope. "I'm my aunt's sole heir. Her house, jewels, money...everything. Why would she leave me her goods? Why not my mother?"

"She must have loved you very much and saw this as a way for you to provide for yourself without depending on others."

"That would be like her. She was adventuresome, so she didn't blink when I told her of my desire to come out West. In fact, she bemoaned the fact she couldn't join me. You know, for one last lark." Her throat thickened, and she swallowed. "I wish you could have known her. She was special."

"Now that you've seen the letter, will you return with me to Boston?"

"I can't. For countless reasons." Her fingers rubbed the envelope. Back and forth. Back and forth. Her chest tightened. Returning to Massachusetts would be a step back, and there were too many people who would try to retain her in their clutches. No. She was content in Oregon. She didn't need wealth to be happy. She had her faith and her friends. That was enough. "I'm sorry you came all this way for nothing."

"Are you willing to explain your reasons?" His voice held curiosity rather than criticism.

"So you can attempt to convince me to change my mind?" She cocked her head and studied his face, searching him for ulterior motives, but finding no evidence.

He shrugged then grinned and put his hand over his heart. "If you feel bad about the fruitlessness of my journey, you owe me some sort of explanation."

"For a detective you're a smooth talker, Mr. Jessop." She giggled. Sparring with him was fun, but she couldn't let him persuade her to go.

"Fine, but then this conversation is over, and you'll get on the next train out of Oregon."

"I've been looking for a change. Perhaps, I'll send a telegram with your answer then remain in this picturesque town."

Her pulse raced. "With the life you must have led, you would soon tire of our sleepy hamlet."

"I doubt it, but thanks for your concern." He lifted an eyebrow and leaned back in the chair. "Now, your reasons?"

"There is nothing that draws me to Boston. In fact, the thought of returning is repugnant. I was never comfortable in society, with its disingenuous nature and constant shuffling of some invisible list of the elite. My parents' search for acceptance by those who disdain families with new money and bartering me in the process."

She heard the bitterness in her voice and cleared her throat. Five years had not wiped away the hurt that her parents considered position more important than her happiness. "The groom they chose for me was a cruel, self-absorbed man who fooled everyone with his behaviors. Should I ever marry, it will be for love, not gain, and certainly not someone such as him. I do not need money or approval by others to feel fulfilled." She crossed her arms and jutted out her chin. "Are those reasons enough for you, Mr. Jessop?"

"Don't you see, by having the money, you can live however you want, without interference. Sell the house and the jewels. You'd be a very rich woman and wouldn't have to work another day in your life."

"But I like my job, serving others, seeing their enjoyment of Mrs. Krause's cooking. Meeting new people." She frowned. "I'm sorry to disappoint you, but my answer is no."

"Okay, so you don't want the money. Give it all away. Makes no nevermind to me, but you need to return to claim it."

"Says who?"

"The provisions of your aunt's will require you to go to Boston. This isn't me or the lawyers talking. Your aunt has said you must do this."

Tears sprang to her eyes. "But why? She knew how miserable I was. Why would she require me do this? Go to the next heir on the list."

Reuben rose, laid his hat on the chair then knelt beside her. He took her fingers in his, his thumb stroking the back of her hand. "Did you trust your aunt?"

Tingles shot up her arm, and she trembled. "Yes." She sniffled.

"Your aunt must have had her reasons, and perhaps they'll become clear when you get to Boston. Please, accompany me back to your home."

She extricated her hands and wrapped them around her middle. Why did life have to be so complicated? What was Auntie thinking when she named Meg as her heir? Why did the woman think she needed to be taken care of? She was doing fine by herself. She'd become part of a community who loved her and where she could be her own person without worrying what others thought.

But the money would make living easier. She'd no longer have to scrimp and save. She could purchase a home of her own and not have to share space with others. Would the newfound wealth be worth the difficulties she was sure to experience in Boston?

Oh, Aunt Ida, why did you put me in this position?

Legacy of Love

Chapter Five

Why did she have to be so cute when she was angry? Reuben rubbed his jaw. He needed to keep his mind on the task, but her pouty lips when she told him no made it difficult to concentrate. The job to get her across the country was supposed to be easy, but so far it had been anything but. He'd thought it might require a little persuasion, but it appeared his mission would take longer to complete than even Allan Pinkerton estimated.

Reuben clenched his fists. Lots of parents arranged their daughters' marriages, but if what Meg was saying was true, her folks had picked a loser. Hadn't they performed their due diligence about their future son-in-law? She'd said he was cruel. Did that mean he'd physically accosted her?

It was tempting to contact the home office to get them to do a background check on the guy, but there was no reason other than his own curiosity. And personal feelings had no place in an assignment. Which took him right back to problem number one—her beauty. Were the men of Spruce Hill blind, or had she turned down numerous proposals from the male population?

Her aunt's money would allow Meg to do whatever she wanted, give her an independence few women had. Why did she reject the opportunity? Being wealthy would enable her to thumb her nose at the society she abhorred as well as the man she despised. Seemed like a logical decision to make, but she was allowing emotions to cloud her judgment. He had to help her see her way clear.

"Meg, I understand why you're upset. You've lost a loved one, someone who supported you, and now you have to make an arduous journey and potentially see people you'd rather not. But think about how the money will change your life for the better. You said you like your job and want to work. You can still do that, but you can ensure your aunt's legacy will be used for something you care about."

He squeezed her arm, and tingles warmed his hand. He rose and made his way back to the chair unsuccessfully trying to ignore the sensation. "I'm not a lawyer, but I would imagine that if you turn down the inheritance, the courts will get involved, which would be a perfectly good waste of the funds. And the person or persons who end up with the bequest may use the money in ways you don't like."

"I don't care." She lifted tear-filled eyes to him. "I don't need her money to be happy. How many times do I have to say that before you'll believe me? Riches don't bring happiness. In fact, from what I've experienced, affluence creates added responsibilities and stress. No, thank you."

"It's only been five years since you left. You're letting your fear of what was destroy what could be. Yes, your parents chose a man you shouldn't have had to marry, but did you try to discuss the situation with them? Give them examples of his cruelty? They wanted to see you provided for, to be taken care of. Can you fault them for that?"

Her eyes widened, and her mouth twisted. She jumped to her feet. "Have you not heard a word I've said? My well-being had nothing to do with their actions. The match was strictly for the good of the family name. You seem to be full of suggestions and solutions, yet you speak without having witnessed the situation. I don't appreciate you judging my decision to take my future into my own hands." She blew out a deep breath. "And yes, I did try to discuss the matter with my parents. They were not interested in anything I had to say."

She gestured toward the door. "This conversation is over. Again, I'm sorry you came to Oregon on a wasted trip, but I refuse to return to Boston. My life is here, and my aunt's worldly goods can be tossed into the ocean for all I care."

Reuben's stomach tightened. He'd insulted and upset her again. Two days in her presence, and he'd become an inarticulate oaf. "Wait. Miss Underwood. I'm sorry. I came here to gain your forgiveness, and I've further antagonized you."

Gaze narrow and piercing, she froze.

He raked his fingers through his hair. "Please, sit down, and let's talk about this rationally. I have heard what you told me, and I'm sorry for what happened to you. But I've been given the task of convincing you to return to Boston, and I'd like you to hear me out. I know this is a difficult decision for you, but how can you make it properly if you don't examine all the angles?"

"Angles?" Her head tilted.

"Yes, the pros and cons, the good reasons and the not-so-good reasons. By considering all the possibilities, you'll know you've made an educated choice, one that you won't later regret, whatever the outcome."

She stared at him, nibbling her lower lip as she seemed to think about his offer.

His heart thundered in his chest as he met her gaze. Would he be bested by a petite young waitress and fail at his mission? He'd had less trouble apprehending bandits and bank robbers. "Miss Underwood? Please, let me help you make your decision. I promise not to try to sway you toward returning."

"Why? Will you get paid even if I stay in Oregon and turn down the inheritance?"

He shrugged. "My salary isn't impacted by the success or failure of a mission, but personally I think your aunt's bequest is a good thing for you." He held up his hand as she opened her mouth to respond. "Let me finish. But what I think doesn't matter. However, this is one of the most important decisions you may ever make, and it shouldn't be done quickly or lightly."

"You barely know me. Why would you do this? You could take my answer, get back on the train, and be home by Thanksgiving. Doesn't your family miss you?"

"Let me get to know you. My parents are dead, and I see my brother often enough, so the holiday is of no consequence." She was right to wonder why he was so insistent. But something inside said she needed his guidance. No, that wasn't right. She needed God's guidance. "Are you a believer, Miss Underwood? If so, you might consider praying about your decision."

Her face pinked, and she nodded. "I am a Christian, and your point is well taken."

Reuben rocked on his heels. "How about this...you have until Christmas to prove to me why you should stay here in Oregon and forsake your aunt's gift. If you've convinced me by that time, I'll leave and never bother you again. Deal?"

She smiled and extended her arm. "Deal."

Grinning, he shook her hand, her cool palm nestling perfectly in his. Would he be able to remain aloof and focused on the job during the next five weeks? Time would tell.

Legacy of Love

Chapter Six

From the kitchen the clatter of pots and pans filtered into the Staghead's dining room. Meg shook her head at the noise. The restaurant wasn't a fine dining establishment, but the patrons should be able to eat their meals without a cacophony. She stifled the desire to go see what had happened, but Mrs. Krause would deal with their temporary dishwasher.

After shaking hands with Reuben yesterday to seal their agreement and obtaining Mrs. Krause's permission, she'd invited him to walk in her shoes for a day by working at the restaurant. He'd jumped at the chance so fast she didn't have time to second-guess her idea. His face had lit up like a child's on Christmas morning.

Now, she'd have the handsome agent underfoot for hours. Worse, with the tight quarters in the kitchen, she'd had to squeeze past him several times, his muscular form too close for comfort. Her cheeks heated, and she blew out a breath. The five weeks before he left were going to be the longest in her life.

He'd been solicitous and teasing since he'd arrived. Retrieving supplies for her that she normally would have stood on a chair to reach. Lifting and moving heavy items for her and Mrs. Krause, who was already treating him like a long-lost son. He'd tugged on Meg's ponytail then pointed at the cook with a look of innocence when Meg turned around. He was becoming entirely too familiar.

A smile on her face, Meg walked to Bethany Spencer's table. "What can I get you today?"

"I'm starving. How about the fried chicken and a cup of coffee? That should hold me until dinner."

Meg wrote the order on a slip of paper. "Busy day at the mill?"

Bethany nodded. "Yes, and I shouldn't have escaped, but the numbers were starting to swim in front of me, so I decided a break was in order." She crossed her arms. "I don't put stock in rumors, but I've heard one too many times to ignore. Are you moving to Boston? I'd hate to see you go."

"The curse of living in a small town. No, I'm not moving to Boston."

"You're not surprised about the gossip, right? From what I hear, the man blurted out the invitation in the middle of the restaurant."

"True." She frowned. "But I turned him down. Didn't folks hear that?"

"Probably, but why is the good-looking courier still here?" Bethany jerked her head toward the kitchen. "And so close. Seems like he didn't take no for an answer."

"I'd better put in your order." Meg pursed her lips. "I'll be back with your coffee." She whirled and hurried to the kitchen. The busyness of summer was gone, and the long, cold nights of winter were approaching. She should have known the town would be buzzing with Mr. Jes— Reuben's presence.

He insisted she use his given name if they were to get to know one another, and she liked the way it felt on her lips. She shook her head as she entered the kitchen then grabbed the pot from the stove and poured the dark liquid into a mug. She looked at the vacant spot in front of the sink. "Where's—"

"Did you miss me?" Reuben filled the back doorway, sunlight creating a halo around him.

Her breath hitched, and she nearly dropped Bethany's drink. "What? No. Thought perhaps the job was too much for you, and you'd skedaddled."

A chuckle rumbled in his chest, and he executed a mock salute. "Not a chance. I'm caught up with my chores, ma'am. Is there anything I can do to help you? Perhaps wait tables?"

"No." She handed Bethany's order to Mrs. Krause. "This is the last one. Everyone else is finishing up their meal or has gone." She rotated her neck to ease the stiffness. "I'm bushed. Good crowd today."

Mrs. Krause nodded and dredged the chicken parts in flour then slipped them into the iron skillet. Sizzling, their aroma filled the kitchen. "Ja. They want to catch a glimpse of our mystery man." She chuckled. "Too bad I kept him back here working. Perhaps the customers will keep coming until they're satisfied."

"You're a sly one, Mrs. Krause." Meg giggled. She glanced at Reuben who was staring at her, a cheeky grin on his face and his blue gaze sparkling. Her pulse quickened, and she held up the coffee mug. "Better deliver this."

She rushed from the kitchen, the heat on her face having nothing to do with the temperature in the room. "Here you go, Bethany. Your lunch will be ready shortly."

Bethany picked up the mug and inhaled deeply. "No hurry. I'm going to enjoy my coffee and the view." She rolled her eyes toward the kitchen then winked.

Meg didn't have to turn around to know that Reuben stood in the doorway, head and shoulders above the swinging door that separated the dining room and the kitchen.

The front door opened, and Sheriff Hobbs stepped inside. He removed his hat and nodded. "Bethany. Meg. How are you ladies today?"

"Doing fine, Sheriff. What can I get you?"

"Coffee, and a piece of whatever pie Mrs. Krause made today."

"Coming right up." Meg headed to the kitchen. Reuben no longer blocked the doorway, so she grabbed the sheriff's order then hurried back to set the items on the table. "Enjoy."

"I plan to. Mrs. Krause makes the best pie I've ever had." He laid his hand on Meg's arm. "Listen, as long as people are obeying the law, what they do is none of my business. However, protectin' people is also part of my job." He leveled his gaze on her. "I've got plenty of contacts, and I can do a background check on our new friend. Find out if what he's saying is true. Would you like me to do that?"

Tension seeped from Meg's shoulders, and she sagged. "Thank you, Sheriff. That would set my mind at ease."

***

Sweat streamed down Reuben's face and stuck his shirt to his back as he scrubbed one of Mrs. Krause's huge stew pots. His muscles bunched. Who knew washing dishes was such a strenuous job? His fingertips were wrinkled from being in the hot water for so long.

The rich scent of chicken frying surrounded him, and his stomach gurgled. How could he be hungry again? The German woman had been plying him with food all day, despite her initial suspicions. She'd stared him down until he'd squirmed and told her he'd answer any and all of her questions. After quizzing him for several minutes, she'd put him to work, but every couple of hours, she'd hand him another delectable piece of food.

Meg was right about her estimation of the town. To their own, they were warm, friendly, and protective. Mrs. Krause had made her feelings about his arrival clear: that if he hurt the young woman, he would pay a price.

Whistling "In the Sweet By and By," he rubbed at a stubborn spot of food clinging to the pot.

"And to what do we owe this chipper mood?" Mrs. Krause's voice held a smile.

Reuben turned and glanced at the cook; his hands still dunked in the water. "Crazy as it seems, I'm more relaxed than I've been in months, and I'm enjoying the satisfaction of a job well done."

She held out a plate of fried chicken. "Honest hard work is always gratifying. Take a break. I heard your stomach."

His face warmed, and he dried his hands before taking the proffered meal. He leaned against the counter and lifted the steaming food to his nose. Inhaling, he closed his eyes and sighed. "You are too good to me, Mrs. Krause."

"Yes, I am."

His eyes flew open, and he studied her impassive expression. Was she teasing or warning him? "Well, I won't let you down."

"It's not me I'm worried about."

"Yes, ma'am. And I promise you I won't hurt Meg...er...Miss Underwood." He took a tentative bite of the meat, and flavor exploded in his mouth. Swallowing, he moaned. "First of all, as a Pinkerton agent, I'm sworn to protect and to serve. Besides that, it's not in my nature to take advantage of or bring grief to young women. But thirdly, I believe that if I did anything to her, there are many people in this town I'd have to answer to...if I managed to get out of here alive."

She nodded. "I'm glad you understand the situation."

He polished off the food, tossed the bones into the trash, and then set aside the plate. He washed his hands and went back to scouring the stubborn pot.

The door swung open, and Meg came into the room, snatched Bethany's order and left. Moments later she returned. "We're done." Her ponytail had slipped, and strands of hair dangled on each side of her face. Fatigue lines creased her forehead, and her shoulders slumped.

"You earned your keep today. Folks kept you hopping."

"They sure did, but you were the main attraction." She dug coins from her apron pocket. "Made for good tips. Wonder how long it will last."

"Glad to help." He rinsed the pot he'd finally managed to get clean and stacked it on the drain rack. "You two ladies should both put up your feet and let me clean up in here. Or I could rustle you up something to eat."

Mrs. Krause waved her hand in a dismissive gesture. "I'll get something later. I want to check my inventory. I'll be in the cellar if you need me."

Meg lowered herself on the chair by the door and shook her head. "I'm not hungry either, but I will take you up on your offer to sit down." She sent him a saucy smile. "There's nothing I like better than to watch a man work. Very relaxing."

He snorted a laugh then flicked water at her.

"Hey!" She grabbed a towel and dried the moisture from her face. "Guess I deserved that."

"Yes, you did, but I forgive you."

"Gee, thanks." She laid the towel in her lap and leaned her head against the wall. "I'm bushed. Thanks for helping out today."

"My pleasure." He drained the sink then dampened a cloth to mop down the stove.

"Right. You enjoyed washing a bunch of yucky dishes."

"Surprisingly, I did. In fact, Mrs. Krause and I were discussing that before you came into the kitchen. Yes, the work itself is tedious and not very pleasant, but the company is lovely, and it felt good to finish a job the day I started it. Cases can drag on for weeks when I'm tracking bad guys."

"But it must be satisfying when you catch them."

"Absolutely." Reuben finished the stove then wiped the counters. "What do you do during your off hours? You spend a lot of time on your feet."

"I often go to the lighthouse and visit with the keepers, if they're not busy, or sit on the rocks and watch the waves."

"Sounds wonderful. Would you mind if I joined you on your next day off? Working together is nice, but there's not much time for conversation. If we're to get acquainted, we need to spend time together talking."

Her face pinked. "You're going to love the lighthouse, and the view of the sea is breathtaking. The ocean reminds me of God's majesty, and my troubles seem to melt away with the crashing of the waves." A distant look came into her eyes, then she blinked. "I'm off the day after tomorrow."

"Perfect. That will give me another day to wash dishes."

"Oh, how the mighty have fallen. From detective to dishwasher." A smile tugged at her lips. "What would Mr. Pinkerton say to your current predicament?"

"Plenty, I'm sure." He chuckled, and the roses on her cheeks deepened to red. He could get used to making her blush, but he had a mission to accomplish. And he'd be gone by the end of the year. And more importantly, it would never do to get involved with the target of an assignment. Difficult since his heart couldn't seem to remember that rule.

Legacy of Love

Chapter Seven

Basket handle draped over one arm, and the other tucked through the crook in Reuben's elbow, Meg entered the church hall. Mrs. Krause followed, carrying a chocolate cake. The church social was a perfect opportunity to show off the town and its virtues, the best of which was its people. Sheriff Hobbs was handling the background check, but exposing Reuben to her friends would allow them to interact and study his behaviors.

She hated to be so suspicious about the man, but her experience with Tyler had made her skittish about men who seemed too good to be true. They usually were. A smile pinned to her lips, she nodded at the women behind the serving table as she approached. "Here you go, Mrs. Comerford. I brought some chicken stew."

"Lovely. You can set it over there." Ash-blonde hair swept into an elegant chignon, Mrs. Comerford stared at Reuben. "And who do we have here?"

Reuben bowed. "Reuben Jessop at your service, ma'am. You folks know how to lay a spread."

Mrs. Comerford laughed, a loud braying sound that filled the room. "Now, you make sure to get your fill. We always have plenty."

He nodded. "Is there anything I can do to help?"

"No, you enjoy your day with Miss Underwood. She works entirely too hard, so it's nice to see her out with a young man. I hope you will be very happy together."

Meg's face heated. "Uh, no, Mrs. Comerford, we're not seeing each other. He's...er...just visiting."

"If you say so, dear, but I can tell when two people have special feelings." She leaned toward them and whispered, "It's a gift."

"But—"

Reuben nudged her shoulder. "Let's check out the dessert table."

"Good idea." Meg set down the dish and followed Reuben across the room, face still warm. Should she comment on the woman's words or pretend they didn't happen?

"Attending this event was a great idea. I hope to meet many of your friends." Reuben rubbed his jaw and winked. "As long as they don't think we're courting."

Meg sighed. So much for avoiding the previous conversation. She rolled her eyes, and he chuckled, so she poked him. "Rest assured, there will be no confusion among my friends."

"Who will you introduce me to first?" He surveyed the room then glanced at her, eyes sparkling with humor.

Her heart stuttered, and she licked her dry lips. She gestured to a thin man whose balding head towered above the crowd. "You haven't met the preacher yet. How about if we start there?"

"Bringing in the big guns, are you?"

"Funny. No, that was the sheriff, and you've already met."

"Yes, and I'm sure he'll let you know when my background check comes back."

She gaped at him. "How do you know—?"

"Because that's what I would have done if some stranger showed up with a story devised to lure one of the young women in my town to get on a train headed out of town. I'm glad to see him cautious about me. Makes me feel good about the safety of Spruce Hill. I can see why you stayed."

"Yes, Sheriff Hobbs has been like a father to me, but he especially helped me when I first arrived."

They approached the minister, and he extended his arm. "Miss Underwood. Mr. Jessop, I'm Pastor Kearns. It's nice to meet you."

"Thank you, sir." Reuben shook his hand. "A pleasure to be here. In this town and at church. Reminds me of mine back home. With my job, I'm not able to attend regularly, but I go when I can."

"You're with the Pinkerton agency?"

"Yes, sir. I see communication in this town is effective."

Pastor Kearns snickered. "And fast. Almost quicker than the telegraph."

"I'd believe that." Reuben stuffed his hands into his pockets. "I look forward to being here on Sunday with Miss Underwood. She's been introducing me to Spruce Hill."

"Will you be here long?"

"A few weeks, perhaps until Christmas."

"Excellent. That will give us a chance to visit, get to know each other better."

Meg swallowed a smile. If not for his call to be a preacher, Pastor Kearns would have made a fine Pinkerton agent or sheriff. She looked forward to his assessment of Reuben.

Wernicke Webb came alongside them. "Miss Underwood. I've not had a chance to meet our visitor."

"Nice to see you, Mr. Webb. This is Mr. Jessop. He's brought me information from back East and will be staying in town for a bit. I'm sure he'd be delighted to give you a hand at the mill should you need it."

Reuben's eyes widened, and then he seemed to recover. "Yes, I've not worked in a mill before, but I'm trainable." He grinned. "Ask Mrs. Krause."

"I'll consider your offer. Nice to have you in our fair village. Would you like to join me at the table?"

Meg nodded. "Yes, let's sit near Bethany and Mr. Forester." Her friend would be thrilled at the opportunity to interrogate Reuben, and she was happy to let her. It would be fun to see how he reacted.

They grabbed plates and selected from the dozens of dishes displayed then seated themselves at one of the six-foot plank tables. Conversation ebbed and flowed, giving Meg the chance to study Reuben as he spoke with others. Gracious and articulate, he answered question after question, a slight smile on his face. Dressed in a charcoal-colored frock coat with low-cut vest and light-gray slacks, he would have fit in any one of Boston's finest drawing rooms.

At one point, Bethany kicked Meg under the table then wiggled her eyebrows at her when their gazes met. Her face flamed.

The pastor stood and clapped his hands. "The weather is unseasonably warm today, and the Pemberton family has brought their instruments. They will be ready to play in a few minutes, so be sure to make your way outside for dancing.

Meg's heart pounded in her ears. She'd forgotten the socials usually included dancing. Rooted in her chair, she stared at Reuben who rose and held out his hand as he cocked his head. Bethany nudged her leg, and Meg jumped to her feet. Grabbing his hand, she tried to ignore the tingles that shot up her arm.

He led her outside where the musicians were already playing a waltz. Reuben drew her into his arms, and they whirled among the other couples. He smiled at her, and his eyes crinkled in the corners. "You're a fine dancer, Meg. Can I assume this was a regular pastime in Boston?"

"Yes, my friends and I learned at a very young age." Tension drained from her shoulders. "As much as I didn't enjoy the gossip and pandering at soirées, I loved the dancing. Music fills me like nothing else. Wouldn't you agree?"

"I like orchestras, but I prefer the music of God's creation: waves crashing on the shore, wind rustling the leaves, especially before a storm, and rain pattering on dry ground."

"Ah, a man of the outdoors. No wonder you love your job." She sighed. "Picnics or carriage rides were the limit of my time outside. I think that's why I'm drawn to visiting the lighthouse."

"Other than your disagreement with your parents about marriage, did you get along with them?"

"Yes, they tried to do their best by me, and there are many good memories, but I never felt as if I truly belonged. My values are vastly different. As I've told you, wealth means nothing to me, and money is important to them."

"It's difficult when we as children begin to separate from our families, create our own lives." He twirled her then brought her close again.

Gazing at his face, she wanted to believe her thundering pulse was a result of the exertion from dancing, but she knew better.

***

The song finished, but Reuben continued to hold Meg in his arms. She didn't seem inclined to quit dancing, and he was happy to oblige. Seconds later, the trio began to play another waltz, and he smiled. He was in no hurry to break into a polka or square dance. They moved around the room in fluid grace, and during one circuit he caught sight of the sheriff staring at them, arms crossed, a frown on his face.

Sweat sprang out on his forehead, and he loosened his grip. In one glance, the sheriff had made him feel like a guilty schoolboy. He had nothing to hide, but knowing he was under investigation by the man unsettled him.

"Are you okay?" Concern paled Meg's face.

"Yes. My apologies. Your sheriff over there is giving me the evil eye."

She laughed, her eyes shimmering. "He apparently sees you as a threat to my safety."

"He has nothing to worry about."

"Convince me." Her gaze narrowed, but a smile hovered on her mouth.

"Fine." He cleared his throat. "I've got one brother, and we were born and raised on a farm in Pennsylvania. I worked hard doing chores, but my parents saw to it that I went to school and got a good education. When the war came, I joined up..." He swallowed the lump in his throat. "I joined with a buddy of mine."

Meg squeezed his shoulder. "Talk of the war seems to be painful as it is for most of the men who went away. You don't have to tell me."

"It's okay. You deserve to know." He forced a smile. "Anyway, Eddie and I ended up in the Army of the Potomac. We saw a lot of action, but Chancellorsville was the worst. The Union Army took a beating, but he and I lived to tell about it. We both managed to make it to the end of the war intact. The agency offered me a job, and I've been with them ever since."

He fell silent, and they danced for several minutes without talking. Aware of how perfectly she fit in his embrace, he nibbled the inside of his cheek. Why had her parents stooped to an arrangement that upset her? With her beauty, they must have been inundated with prospects. Was there something in the family's background that made her undesirable?

Memories of the conversation he'd had with father after securing work with the agency washed over him. His proud smile when he shared the news of his prospective job. If there had been any indication Dad needed or wanted him to remain on the farm, he'd have turned down Mr. Pinkerton, but he'd given his blessing. As the years passed, and his father aged, guilt nagged him and prompted him to consider going home. "My dad was thrilled I'd found a way to earn a living I love as much as he loved farming."

"How special for you." Her eyes clouded. "I wish my parents had been as understanding."

"Perhaps someday they will."

Her mouth twisted. "You mean if I go home and claim my inheritance."

She tried to pull away, but he tightened his grasp on her hand. "No, I meant my comment as encouragement. Nothing more."

"I'm sorry." She relaxed in his arms. "You've agreed to stay. I shouldn't read meaning into your words."

"No need to apologize. I—"

A tap on his shoulder, then an unfamiliar deep voice spoke in his ear. "Excuse me. May I cut in?"

Meg looked over his shoulder with a smile. "Good afternoon, Tad. I'm glad you could make it."

Reuben's stomach clenched, but he released his hold on her, then bowed. "Certainly. Enjoy your dance." He sauntered to a small table that held several pitchers of water and poured some in a glass. Footsteps sounded behind him, and he turned.

Sheriff Hobbs ambled toward him, a frown on his face.

A sigh escaped, and Reuben clamped his lips together. Let the sheriff make the first move, but something had set him off.

"Jessop. Anything you want to share about why you upset Miss Underwood."

Reuben held his hands up in surrender. "A simple disagreement. She misunderstood something I said, but we'd smoothed over the situation before you sent the cavalry."

"My son."

"Ah. Of course." He shrugged. "She thought I was pushing her to go to Boston. I was not."

The sheriff's eyebrow shot up. "No? But if you don't convince her, you will have failed."

"Yes, but browbeating someone rarely works, and a church social is not the place for a serious discussion."

"I'm glad you recognize that."

"Look, you have no reason to trust me. I understand that, but I don't mean any harm to Meg. I'd like to see her claim the bequest because I believe it would give her the independence she seeks. However, the choice is hers."

Hobbs glared at him for a long moment then gave him a curt nod. "I'll be watching you."

Reuben raised his glass. "I'd expect nothing less." He turned and watched the dancers; his arms bereft of Meg's warm presence. He was a professional lawman. How could he be attracted to the young woman after only eight days? He cast a sidelong glance at the sheriff's glower and schooled his features into what he hoped was a nonchalant expression. If only he could get his heart to remain detached.

Chapter Eight

The salty air stroked Reuben's cheeks as he walked beside Meg. In the distance, the hypnotic rush of ocean waves filtered through the trees. The walk from town to the small home belonging to Jonathan and Amy Powell had been a long trek, but it had given him time to talk to Meg or simply watch her in companionable silence. The deeper they went into the woods, the more tension she seemed to shed. Interesting for a girl raised in the heart of one of America's largest cities. Although not as big as New York or Philadelphia in population or geographic size, Boston was home to over two hundred and fifty thousand people.

They emerged from the forest, and the Powell residence came into view. A quilt hung on the porch railing in front of a pair of wooden rocking chairs. The flower garden had been prepared for the oncoming winter, cleared of leaves and debris, and the perennials cut back. Smoke wafted from the chimney.

The front door opened and a woman, he presumed to be their hostess, smiled and waved. Her cinnamon-colored hair glistened in the waning sunlight. Tall and willowy, she reminded Reuben of the slender wheat stalks that covered the plains. Meg returned the greeting and hurried toward the house. Reuben quickened his pace to join her.

A tall, burly man with blond hair and beard appeared behind the woman, his green eyes guarded. His hand on her shoulder, he seemed to study his guests with something akin to suspicion. Reuben sighed. Would he be subjected to more interrogation over their meal?

"Welcome. You must be Reuben. I'm Amy Powell, and this is my husband, Jonathan. We're so pleased to have you."

Jonathan dipped his head. "Thank you. I look forward to getting to know you." He gestured to the ocean. "A beautiful view."

"We like it. Don't we?" She poked her husband with an elbow, and he grunted.

The bear of a man nodded. "Yep."

Meg stepped onto the porch, and the couple moved into the house. Reuben followed everyone inside, his gaze absorbing the cozy, inviting atmosphere. The heady aroma of baked fish mingled with the earthy fragrance of baked potatoes. The table was set with white china plates patterned with a ring of blue flowers. Glasses were filled with apple cider, and steam rose from the tantalizing food.

Amy gestured to the chairs. "Please, have a seat. We don't stand on ceremony here."

Reuben held Meg's chair then seated himself next to her. The Powells sat across the rustic wooden table. Dishes were passed, and soon his plate was nearly overflowing. He inhaled deeply. "I've had more delicious meals since arriving in Spruce Hill than I've ever experienced."

"Thank you, Mr. Jessop." His hostess blushed. "Are you enjoying your stay?"

"Yes, ma'am. And please call me Reuben." He forked a piece of translucent flaky fish into his mouth and sighed. "Meg has introduced me to many of the sights around the area, and I've been surprised at the diversity. Having never visited the West Coast before, I thought the shoreline would feel like that of North Carolina or Virginia, but it's quite different. Lovely in a stark kind of way."

"I agree." She scooped up some of the fluffy potatoes. "I'm from New York City and was headed for San Francisco, but I ended up here and couldn't be happier." She squeezed her husband's arm, and his expression thawed for a brief second as their eyes met.

"Don't you miss the city? The cultural opportunities? The variety of available items? Entertainment?"

Amy giggled, a bright, tinkling sound reminiscent of wind chimes. She shook her head. "Not in the least. Do I tire of eating fish? Do I occasionally wish I could go to the theater? Perhaps. But not enough to move away. I have the love of a good man and a full life. I wouldn't give it up for anything."

Meg nodded as she stabbed several green beans. "I'm the same way, Amy. Boston was fine while I was growing up, but the slower pace of Spruce Hill is just what I need. And the townspeople are warm and friendly. I'm treated the same as Bethany and Mr. Forester even though I'm not rich like they are. In Boston, society is all about how much money someone has or who they know or are related to." She shuddered. "No, thank you."

Reuben cocked his head. "Mr. Powell..er...Jonathan, were you surprised that Amy wanted to remain here? To give up everything to be a fisherman's wife...no offense meant."

"None taken." Jonathan's baritone voice rumbled in his chest. "I was skeptical that a big-city girl would be content with me." A shadow passed over his face. "And it took a crisis to bring me to my senses, but Amy fits into Spruce Hill as if she was born here." He grinned at his wife. "She's even learned to swim."

Amy swatted her husband's arm. "You can't blame me for not knowing how. I never went to the beach while in New York."

His eyes shone as he glanced at her and chuckled.

Reuben studied the couple then slanted a look at Amy, who watched them, too. He shrugged. Didn't seem possible that anyone could be glad to exchange the advantages of a well-developed city for the isolation of a remote village, but by all appearances the woman seemed to be telling the truth. During the walk to their home, he'd wondered if Meg had coached her friend on what to say to him, but Amy's open expression belied that thought.

They finished their meal, and soon it was time to head back to town. Meg had offered to help Amy with the dishes, but the fisherman's wife had shooed her away, claiming that she and Jonathan could handle the chore after their guests left. The foursome lingered on the front porch for several minutes and made plans to dine together again. By the end of the midday meal, Jonathan had warmed up and talked at length about his fishing business and his parents who were both gone. He'd questioned Reuben about his work, but his queries seemed inquisitive rather than a cross-examination.

"Thanks, again." Reuben lifted his hand in farewell. "I look forward to a day on the boat with you, Jonathan."

"Any time."

He and Meg turned and ambled toward the trees and were soon enveloped in the green canopy of Douglas fir, hemlock, and cedar. As they walked, he cogitated over the hours spent with the Powells. Amy's actions supported her words that she was thrilled to be a member of the Spruce Hill community. Of course, she'd visited her grandparents in San Francisco and would no doubt do so periodically. Perhaps that helped her remain content in Oregon. But Boston was a long journey. Meg would be unable to make the jaunt on a regular basis.

"A penny for your thoughts." Meg bumped his shoulder and grinned.

"They'll cost you more than that." He grinned.

"If I were a betting woman, I'd say you were thinking about what Amy said and how that compares to my situation." She tucked her hands into her skirt pockets.

Reuben gaped at her. Was he that transparent?

"I take it from your expression that I guessed correctly." She laughed. "It wasn't hard to surmise. You're a detective, and it stands to reason you were hoping that clues from Amy would help you figure out how to convince me to return home. She's the only person from the city that I know, so it makes sense your investigation would include speaking with her."

"Brilliant. Pinkerton would love to have you on his staff."

"No, thank you. I'm happy serving people at the restaurant."

"Are you?" He cocked his head. "You're smart and articulate. You could be so much more."

A frown creased her forehead. "Because there are so many employment opportunities for women."

"Well, I...uh—" His face warmed, and he gave himself a mental kick.

She poked his side. "Don't worry. I'm not offended. There aren't a lot of jobs women can have, but I like what I do, make enough money to pay my bills, and can leave the day behind once I'm off work. If I were the owner, I would have responsibilities and stress." She kicked a small stone, and it rattled down the path. "You've lived far and wide and done a lot of exciting things. I know you can't understand my desire to remain here in this tiny corner of the world. But God creates us all differently. That's why lots of people took advantage of the Homestead Act to spread out across the country while others stayed sequestered in their cities."

"I appreciate your willingness to explain your viewpoint. I'm trying to grasp your reasons, but maybe my travels are giving me a blind eye."

Meg covered her eyes. "Perhaps." She laughed and put her hands back into her pockets then skipped ahead of him. She whirled so she was facing him. "You asked me whether I'd prayed about Auntie's bequest. I could ask you the same thing. Have you prayed about your mission? Are you making any sort of attempt to discern what God wants of me? Or are you afraid He'll tell you I'm right where I'm supposed to be?" She wagged her forefinger at him, her porcelain skin shining and a bright smile on her face. "Now, enough serious discussion. Let's enjoy creation and each other's company."

He hurried to catch up with her and stifled the urge to grab her hand as they traversed the trail. She'd not demanded an answer about whether he was praying for her. What would he say if she had? His prayers had been more like pleas for help to maintain his distance. Did those count? Probably not.

When was the last time he'd prayed about his own path? Too many years. For the split second before Mr. Pinkerton had given him this assignment, he'd wondered if a change was on the horizon. Then he'd hopped on the train and never looked back.

As usual. Always moving forward. Always seeking the next case. But at someone else's beckoning. Was it time to consider another life?

Would it be so bad to settle down, to put down roots? Perhaps in a small coastal town guarded by a lighthouse.

Chapter Nine

The last of the diners wandered out the door of the restaurant, and Meg blotted at the perspiration on her face. Another busy lunch. Coins in her apron pocket jingled as she wiped down the tables and chairs in preparation for tomorrow's breakfast. Her customers had been generous. Humming to herself, she put the room to rights then grabbed a broom and began to sweep the floor. Her shoulders ached and her back protested as she cleaned up crumbs and debris. Lying on the couch with a good book was the perfect way to spend the evening.

Footsteps sounded on the porch, and she looked up as Sheriff Hobbs entered. He removed his Stetson and smiled. "Good afternoon. I've got news. Do you have a few minutes?"

She nodded and leaned the broom against the wall then gestured to a nearby table. Her heart pounded. What information did he bring?

He lowered himself in the chair across from her and laid his hat on the table. "I waited until I saw Reuben head out. Will he be back?"

"No. It's Wednesday, so we're closed for dinner. He's done for the day."

"Right." He leaned forward and propped his elbows on his knees. "I've collected what I can about your friend and wanted to let you know that he's a straight-up guy."

Meg cocked her head. "You seem...I don't know...surprised or maybe disappointed."

Sheriff Hobbs chuckled. "Not disappointed, but a bit taken aback. Rarely are people all that they seem. Yet, he is. How much has he told you?"

"He doesn't talk much about the war, but most who were there don't. He said he served in the Union Army and listed a couple of battles. I know he's from Pennsylvania and that his parents still have a farm there. He's been with Pinkerton since shortly after the war."

"That's it?"

Her face heated. "Yes. Should I have pressed him for more?"

"Not necessarily, but I figured you might have."

"We've talked about other things, and I knew you were checking on him. Why ask him questions he might not answer truthfully?"

"Did you ever think he was lying?"

"No, and after Tyler, I can generally get a sense when someone isn't being honest."

The sheriff nodded. "I'm real sorry for what you went through."

She shrugged. "Could have been worse. I found out about him before we married."

"A blessing, for sure." He laced his fingers. "Anyway, about Reuben. He served with distinction and received the Medal of Honor. Got a bunch of commendations from his commanding officers, too. He's a brave fellow and saved many of his fellow soldiers' lives. He received several battlefield promotions and mustered out as a captain. Not bad for a guy who went in as a private."

"He said he was wounded."

"Most men were." Sheriff Hobbs cleared his throat. "There's some society for the Army of the Potomac that formed a couple of years ago, and he received a medal from them for his service. One of his commanding officers worked for Allan Pinkerton during the war and afterward recommended the agency hire Reuben. He's worked some high-profile cases, and he always gets his man, but his last case didn't go well. The guy who he often partnered with was killed during a shootout."

Meg's hand flew to her mouth. "Oh, no. How awful. Was Reuben injured?"

"No, and initially, there was some question as to his culpability in what happened. Pinkerton conducted the investigation himself and determined our friend wasn't at fault. But I would imagine Reuben revisits the event in his mind, rolling it over and over to figure out what he could have done differently. To lose a partner is one thing, but this man was also a friend. They'd known each other a long time and went through the war together."

Tears sprang to her eyes. "He told me he'd joined with a friend named Eddie Watkins, but he didn't tell me about the man's death. How tragic."

"Listen, Meg. It's none of my business, but I wanted to remind you that as an agent, Reuben never stays in one place. He has no home to speak of. Once a case is finished, he moves on to the next assignment."

"Yes, it's the very nature of his job. Why do you feel you need to caution me about that?"

"Well, in case you've got any designs on him."

Meg reared back. "What? Designs on the man? I don't know where you would have gotten an idea like that, but you needn't worry. I'm simply showing *Mister* Jessop around the area to convince him that I have thought through my decision to remain in Spruce Hill and will not accompany him to Boston to claim my inheritance. I've no interest in wealth, but he seemed adamant that I prove my point. Our spending time together is nothing more than a business arrangement."

Sheriff Hobbs held up his hands. "Okay, okay. No need to get a bee in your bonnet. I'm just doing my job."

"By prying into my personal life?"

"Maybe I crossed a line, but it's only because I don't want to see you get hurt again. Forgive me."

She blew out a deep breath and rubbed the edge of the table. "Sorry. I guess I overreacted. As I said, my goal is to convince him I'm making a fully informed choice and that he needs to leave without me.

End of story, and I'll never see him again." She pressed her lips together. Why did that thought cause her stomach to hollow with disappointment?

***

Leaves crunched underfoot as Reuben tromped through the forest. The scent of earthy decay wafted toward him with every footstep. Birds chirped overhead, and chipmunks scurried among the shrubbery. The distant sound of waves crashing told him he'd almost arrived at his destination: the Powells' cabin.

Mrs. Powell, or Amy as she insisted on being called, had come to town the previous day and invited him for a visit. Eager to explore her reasons for exchanging the city life for that of a fisherman's wife, he'd jumped at the chance. His stomach rumbled, and he grinned. That and the opportunity to partake of her delicious food.

He stepped into the clearing, and movement to the left caught his attention. Seated on a tired crate that looked like it wouldn't hold the man's weight, Jonathan was mending a net, his beefy hands more dexterous than Reuben would have thought. The man looked up and nodded then bent over his work again. Apparently, he wouldn't be joining his wife and her guest.

Torn between whether he should talk to Jonathan or head to the cabin, he remained rooted in position.

"Reuben!" Amy peeked around the edge of the house and waved. "I'm back here. Why don't you join me?"

He nodded and trotted alongside the home then ducked into the backyard. She'd set three chairs around a small wooden table which held a platter of sandwiches, a pitcher of water, and three glasses. "Jonathan?"

She shrugged. "Maybe. He's not one for jawing, but he might join us if he finishes the net."

"The work is never done, is it? He's either preparing to fish, catching the fish, or canning the fish."

"Our lives do revolve around those slippery creatures." She sat down and gestured to the nearest chair. "I'm not hungry, but help yourself." She filled two of the glasses then picked up one and took a sip.

"Thank you." He filled his plate and seated himself. "I was pleased to get your invitation. Your property is gorgeous, and I've fallen in love with the view. Despite Pennsylvania's proximity to the coast, I've had few opportunities to visit the sea. There's something mesmerizing about it."

"Indeed. And having been raised visiting the Atlantic Ocean, I was surprised at how different the Pacific coast is. I never tire of looking at it and watching the waves." She cradled her glass and squinted at him. "I thought you might want to talk more about my decision to stay in Spruce Hill in light of Meg's unwillingness to return to Boston."

He chuckled. "Am I that obvious?"

She shrugged. "Let me share my thoughts, then you are welcome to ask as many questions as you'd like."

"All right."

"Family is important. I'm well aware of that because I lost my parents at a fairly young age and was raised by my grandparents. But I can also understand Meg's reticence because I, too, was destined for an arranged marriage. I knew it was my duty, but frankly, my heart wasn't in the prospect of marrying someone I'd never met. When Jonathan came into my life, I knew I couldn't follow through with going to San Francisco. I've not regretted my decision for one minute." She drank some water. "Granted, less than a year has passed since my arrival, so perhaps you think not enough time has passed for those feelings to surface, but trust me when I tell you that our lives, though happy, are not always easy."

"But the area is so remote. Don't you get lonely?"

"Sometimes, especially when Jonathan has to be out for several days, but then I go into town and stay with friends."

"Friends aren't the same as family."

"True, but family isn't always about blood, and the town has become my family. I know you travel a lot with your job, but don't you have a friend who is closer than a brother?"

The image of Eddie's face flashed into Reuben's mind, and his chest tightened. He nodded and licked his lips. "Yes, but he's gone now, so there's no one now."

She squeezed his arm: her eyes clouded. "I'm sorry."

He nodded and cleared his throat. "Suffice it to say, I can relate to what you're saying about family, but what about the wealth? Not to be crass, but I've heard you were quite well to do. You've said your life with

Jonathan can be hard at times. I assume that's because money is tight? Don't you resent the fact that you have to work so hard to make ends meet?"

"One would think so, but no. Because we work so hard, I appreciate every cent we earn. I receive great satisfaction from making my own way and partnering with Jonathan."

"But you could have so much more."

A smile lit her face, and she shook her head. "But I have everything I need. We can put food on the table and clothes on our back. And we have more than enough love for one lifetime. He completes me in a way no one else ever has." She set down her glass. "I don't know what else I can say to convince you that if Meg feels as I do, she doesn't need the inheritance to be happy. Why do you feel the need to compel her to obtain it?"

"As I told the sheriff and Meg, having the kind of wealth her aunt has left her will allow her the independence she seeks. But even if I have no opinion on what she should do, I've been tasked with escorting her to Boston, and that's what I aim to do."

"Even against her wishes?"

His cheeks heated. "Well, no. That's why I'm still here."

"Meg's a grown woman. Why can't you believe that she knows what she wants? She said no. Shouldn't you respect her answer? Or has your assignment become a bit personal? She's a beautiful, intelligent woman."

"I do respect her." Did he? Amy's words cut deeply. Was he assuming that Meg didn't really comprehend what she was rejecting? And what about Amy's assertion that his feelings had become involved? Did she perceive his attraction to Meg? Attraction that he could never follow through on. Nothing could come of their relationship. He was not a man to settle down, and she'd made it clear she wasn't going anywhere.

His throat closed in disappointment.

Legacy of Love

Chapter Ten

Children's voices and laughter filled the backyard of the orphanage, and Meg smiled at the youngsters' happy faces. One of her favorite times of the week was the hours she spent volunteering at the home. Today she'd brought Reuben to give him a glimpse into another facet of her life. When she suggested the outing to share another reason why she couldn't go to Boston, a look of horror had crossed his features before he'd slid an impassive expression into place. Apparently, he was less terrified of outlaws than kids.

With a chuckle, she'd informed him that his gun would be checked at the door as a safety precaution. He'd responded that he never went without the weapon, but she assured him the children were not a threat. With a chuckle, he'd asked her if she was sure about that assertion. She grinned at the memory of his smirk.

Beside her, he stood ramrod straight, his gaze narrow as he surveyed the playground. She nudged his shoulder. "Relax and look like you're enjoying yourself."

He blew out a loud breath, removed his hat, and ran his fingers through his hair.

She gestured to a small child hunkered down in the far corner drawing in the dirt with a stick. "Over there. Lemuel is by himself. That's a perfect chance to inaugurate you into working with children. We're not supposed to have favorites, but he's such a dear. I love playing with him." She tucked her hand in the crook of Reuben's elbow, pausing at the warmth under her fingers. "We'll go together, and I'll keep you safe."

"Funny."

With a saucy smile, she tugged him toward the child. "Just follow my lead, and you'll be fine."

They threaded their way between the other children and approached the little boy who squatted over a patch of dirt. The tip of his tongue peeked out of his mouth as he frowned in concentration over his artwork.

Meg bent and stroked the child's glossy black hair. "Hi, Lem. How are you today?"

He dropped the stick and stood then wrapped his arms around her legs. "Miss Meg. You're here."

Her heart swelled at the feel of his tiny body embracing her knees. She'd have taken him home in a trice if the Quinns' didn't require the children to be placed with married couples. "And I brought a friend. Would you like to meet him?"

Lem's gaze shot toward Reuben, and he studied the lawman with the seriousness of a judge at sentencing. He tucked his thumb in his mouth and pressed closer to her.

Legacy of Love

She knelt and drew the child into her arms. "I think you'll like him. He's a very nice man." She looked at Reuben and wiggled her eyebrows. "Even though he's somewhat rough around the edges."

"Hey—"

Meg yanked on Reuben's hand, and he knelt beside her. She pulled Lem's thumb from his mouth then kissed the back of his hand. "We'll sit with you while you draw. Will that be all right?"

Another calculating look at Reuben, and Lem nodded. He patted the agent's shoulder then pointed to a spot near his so-called artwork. "You sit there."

"Uh, okay." Reuben scooted to where Lem had indicated and sat down.

In a flash, the child crawled into the lawman's lap, picked up his stick, and resumed drawing.

Eyes wide, Reuben stared at the little boy, and Meg swallowed a giggle. She tucked her skirts underneath herself and settled onto the ground. Her parents would be aghast to see her in such a position. Another reason returning to Boston was out of the question. They'd never understood her desire to spend time with those less fortunate, telling her to choose a different way to serve.

She glanced at the two in front of her. Lem still gripped the stick, but Reuben had cupped his hand around the little boy's fist guiding his motions. Both were so intent on their task, they seemed oblivious to her presence.

Sunlight glinted off Reuben's hair, and the muscles under his shirt bunched as he moved. The aroma of leather, sweat, and a scent unique to him wafted toward her. She closed her eyes and inhaled. Her heart hammered. Her eyes flew open, and her face heated. What was she doing? Her life was in Spruce Hill. His was...not.

"Finished." Lem climbed off Reuben's lap and walked to her. "Mr. Reuben helped me. Come look."

Blinking several times to clear her thoughts, she nodded and rose then smoothed her skirts, giving herself time to cool her cheeks. She looked at the dirt and gaped. They'd reproduced a ranch, complete with stick cows and cowboys. "Well, aren't you talented? That's quite good." She cocked her head. "Another hidden talent, Reuben?"

He shrugged, but appeared pleased. "Not much to do in front of the campfire."

"Perhaps when you retire from catching bad guys, you can become an artist."

"Scribbling in the soil is one thing, working on a canvas quite another."

"I'm impressed." Her stomach rumbled, and she glanced at the watch pinned to her bodice. "I'm famished. The kids will be going down for their naps shortly, so now is as good a time as any to make our exit." She hugged Lem. "Mister Reuben and I have to leave, but we'll see you next week."

"Okay. Thanks for coming."

She waved and headed toward the house, tears pricking the backs of her eyes. As much as she enjoyed her time with the children, leaving was bittersweet. They were well taken care of by the Quinns and seemed happy, but Lem burrowed himself deeper in her heart each visit, making subsequent departures harder.

They climbed into the wagon, and Reuben drove it to the far end of town where a small gazebo was surrounded by flower gardens. Used for outdoor concerts and other events, the octagonal-shaped pavilion was a popular location for picnickers. To her relief it was empty. He climbed down then helped her out, his hands warm and firm on her waist. He reached into the back of the conveyance and grabbed the basket Mrs. Krause had packed.

He pretended to stagger under the weight of the hamper then set it on the floor. "We could have fed the kids with what she's provided."

"She is generous." Meg lowered herself next to the basket and removed the towel covering its contents. Savory and sweet smells emanated from inside, and she began to unload the food. "Fried chicken, potato-and-cucumber salad, corn bread, and apple crisp. A bottle of apple cider, too."

Reuben rubbed his hands together. "I love that woman."

Meg giggled as they served themselves. "And apparently, she loves you, too. You're right about enough for the children." She sighed as they ate in companionable silence. A perfect day. The weather was gorgeous. She'd seen Lem, and now she was enjoying the company of a handsome man who made her laugh. She wouldn't think about the fact theirs was a business relationship. For now, she'd immerse herself in the moment.

Hoofbeats thundered toward them, and her head whipped toward the sound.

Reuben jumped to his feet and unholstered his gun. Gripping it in his right hand, he gestured for her to get behind him.

She dropped her plate with a clatter and rushed to do his bidding. Her heart threatened to jump from her chest. She peered over his shoulder at the approaching rider. Did whoever it was really mean them harm?

The sleek bay horse halted, its sides heaving. The man dismounted and removed his hat.

"Tyler!" A wave of nausea swept over Meg, and dizziness almost sent her to the ground. She grabbed Reuben's shoulder to keep from falling as she gaped at her ex-fiancé. How had he found her?

Tyler bowed, an arrogant sneer on his face. He raked his gaze over her and Reuben. "Doesn't this look cozy."

Gun still cocked, Reuben glared at the man. "Who are you and what do you want?"

"Forgive my manners. Tyler Armory, at your service. The lovely women you're dining with is my fiancée."

"Fiancée?" Bewilderment creased Reuben's brow.

Meg's stomach dropped. This wasn't happening. Anger replaced her fear, and she straightened her spine. "Ex-fiancée, Tyler. You have no hold over me anymore. I don't know what you're up to, but whatever it is won't work, so you may as well go home."

"Come now, Meg, you're overreacting. You were always such a suspicious woman." His eyes glittered, his voice oily. "You've had your fun living on your own in the Wild West. It's time to come home to your proper place as my wife. Despite your ridiculous behavior, I'm still willing to marry you."

She snorted a laugh and stepped out from behind Reuben. "*Willing* to marry me? Who's being ridiculous now? I will never marry you, Tyler, and I thought I made that clear when I broke our engagement. I returned your ring. How much more explicit must I be?"

"You're confused. I understand. Let's go to that charming restaurant I saw on my way into town and talk about this." His gaze slid to Reuben. "Without your interfering friend."

She shook her head, glad her dress hid her quaking knees. Could he really force her to marry him? "No, Tyler. There's nothing to discuss. Please leave."

His face darkened, and he moved toward them.

Reuben lifted the gun, aiming it at Tyler's heart. "You heard the lady. She's not interested in anything you have to say. I suggest you get on your horse and go back where you came from."

"You wouldn't shoot me."

"*Want* to bet on that?" He gestured toward the horse. "If Miss Underwood had wanted to marry you, she'd have done so. Showing up here with your condescending attitude is no way to endear her to you. You've yet to mention loving her, but even if you did, she could never marry a stuffed shirt like you."

"You know nothing about me."

"I've seen enough guys like you that I know exactly who you are. The eastbound train leaves first thing in the morning. I suggest you're on it."

Licking her dry lips, Meg trembled. How did Tyler find her? The only people who knew her location were Reuben and Mr. Pinkerton.

Tyler pointed at them, his face dark with rage. "This is not over. You'll come to your senses, Meg, and when you do, I'll be waiting for you." Clamping his hat on his head, he stalked to his horse, and climbed into the saddle, then swung the horse around and trotted away.

She swayed and swallowed the lump in her throat. Reuben wrapped his arm around her shoulder to steady her, and she leaned into him. If she'd been alone when Tyler found her, she had no doubt he would have taken her by force. "Thank you. If you hadn't been here—"

Reuben put a finger to her lips then drew her into an embrace and patted her back. "You're safe now."

Safer than she'd ever been.

Chapter Eleven

Potato and carrot chunks sizzled in the iron skillet, and Meg sprinkled salt and pepper over the vegetables, their aroma filling the tiny kitchen and mingling with the scent of roasting ham. Reuben sat at the table shucking corn, whistling as he worked. She'd invited him, Mrs. Krause, Bessie, one of the other girls in the boarding house, and some of the folks from church, who didn't have family, to celebrate Thanksgiving. He'd immediately volunteered to help her with cooking for the crowd. Bessie had joined them for most of the morning, then ducked out to take some food to a friend who wasn't feeling well.

Reuben looked up and caught her staring at him. He winked, and her face heated. She cleared her throat. "You seem to be an old hand at kitchen work."

"I didn't have much choice while growing up, but now I enjoy cooking. After my mom died, my dad kind of went into a trance. He was so grief-stricken, it was all he could do to get through each day. He stopped eating or doing any chores around the house, so I had to take care of things. My brother was only three."

Tears welled in her eyes, and she blinked them away. "How old were you?"

"Eight years old."

"I'm sorry. That must have been difficult. Almost like losing both parents."

He nodded. "In the beginning the townspeople brought meals to us, but as the weeks turned into months, that slowed until it stopped. They couldn't feed us forever. They had their own families. Besides, learning how to cook, clean our clothes, and other tasks was good for me. Good skills to have, especially since I'm on my own."

"You'll make someone a good wife." She sent him a cheeky grin.

With a chuckle, he wagged an ear of corn at her and puffed out his chest. "You laugh, but I'm quite a catch."

"That you are."

"Anyway, eventually Dad came back, not all at once, but as if he were waking from a deep sleep, until we were able to handle chores together. Sadness lurked in his eyes until the day he died two years ago. I wished he'd found another wife. He deserved to be happy after more than twenty years of being alone."

"Sounds like he loved your mother very much. Perhaps he didn't feel anyone else could take her place."

"Yes, that's what he said. I guess I didn't believe him." He laid down the corn and reached for another piece and began to strip the husk. "Didn't mean to create a somber mood."

"You didn't. Thanksgiving is a time to remember family. At least it is for me." She squeezed his arm. "In between doing chores, did you wonder what you'd do when you grew up?"

"I knew I didn't want to farm, but I liked being around the horses. I thought I might work on a ranch, but then the war came and changed my plans."

"Everyone's lives were turned upside down. Nothing is the same since then." She stirred the vegetables, and they crackled and popped in the pan. "I was in my teens when the war broke out, but I still remember my friend's brothers, fathers, and uncles heading off. Selfishly, I was glad my father was too old to go and that I didn't have a brother."

"I understand the feeling. I was relieved my brother was too young." He picked silk strands from between the kernels. "You're an only child. Was it lonely for you?"

"Not really. I had lots of friends."

"Do you miss them?"

"You mean enough to return to Boston?" She narrowed her gaze at him, and he flushed. She grinned and shook her wooden spoon at him. "I know what you're trying to do, and it won't work."

"You can't blame me for trying. My mission hasn't changed." He leaned forward. "I know what you didn't like about Massachusetts. Is there anything you remember with fondness?"

"I mentioned my friends. Some were closer than others. And summers were glorious. We had a lovely home on Cape Cod that overlooked the ocean. Before the temperatures got too hot, we'd pack up the household and head to the cottage. The days were long and relaxing. Father would spend the first two weeks with us then return to the city and come visit on the weekends sometimes."

"Cottage? I have a feeling your summer place is bigger than my family's cabin."

"Possibly, but with only three bedrooms, a kitchen, and living room there was hardly room to turn around. We left the servants at home, except Cook. Mother hates to prepare meals. There didn't seem to be the worry of society protocols. We could just be a family." She sighed. "That was nice."

"What about the winters? I've heard they can be harsh."

Memories of cold afternoons building snowmen and making snow angels washed over her, and she smiled. "Harsh, yes, and difficult for adults who had to deal with inclement weather, but for a young girl, it was lovely. We went sledding and played outside for hours."

"Vastly different from the Oregon Coast."

She wrinkled her nose. "Yes, we're hard-pressed to get more than a foot or so. Our precipitation is mostly rain. Lots of clouds, too. But we find tasks and activities to amuse ourselves, and before long spring has arrived with summer not far behind."

"If you took the inheritance, you could travel to California for the winter months giving you the best of both. Or if you miss snow, you could return to Boston each winter."

"Nice try, the mountains have plenty of snow if I have a hankering to see some."

He tossed the last ear of corn into the bowl and stood. Stretching, the muscles under his shirt rippled.

Meg's pulse raced, and she turned back to the stove. Fortunately, the vegetables were finished, so she'd have something to do rather than stare at Reuben. Her heart pounded. My, but he was a good-looking man. Gracious, too. He wasn't pushing her to go home. More like nudging. Asking her to consider the situation, taking into account happy memories. Allowing her to rub away the hurt that lingered. Would she be able to remain impartial as she showed him more of her beautiful state?

***

Reuben carried the bowl of shucked corn to the counter beside the stove. "You can have your snow. I've had enough cold to last a lifetime." He shivered. "I grew up in the Allegheny Mountains, near Lake Erie. Our winters are long, and we can get six to eight feet of snow."

"More than Boston." She slid the corn into the pot of boiling water. "Did you play in it while growing up?" Her smile faltered. "I know your life was difficult, but did you have a chance for fun?"

"Sure, I did, but as an adult, I see how the snow and ice disrupt travel and create difficulties."

"True, but have you ever awakened in the morning after a fresh snowfall? You had no idea the storm was coming, and unlike rain, the snow doesn't make noise." Her eyes glowed. "Everything is white and clean, and the sun shimmers on the ice crystals. It's magnificent."

Her joy was palpable, and he tried not to stare. She was so easy to talk with that he'd shared his boyhood woes, something he'd never done with anyone, even Eddie. Mr. Pinkerton knew the bare facts because Reuben had been required to tell the detective his life story during his interview. The man needed to know if there was anything in his past that would have created problems, impacted a mission, or could have been used against him.

Pinkerton had scribbled some notes, grunted in acknowledgment, then moved on to the next question. Businesslike. Clinical. But here with Meg, the conversation had been gently probing. She seemed to be honestly interested, and when he'd mentioned his losses, tears had filled her eyes. She'd shared his grief, and instead of the usual sharp needles of pain that pricked his heart when he remembered his parents, the hurt was only a deep throb.

"Don't you think?" Meg looked at him, confusion in her eyes.

"I'm sorry, what?" She'd apparently said something, and he'd been so caught up in memories, he'd missed her words.

"I asked whether you'd ever taken a walk after a fresh snowfall?"

"Not that I recall." He shook his head. "Or at least not for the purpose of simply trudging through the drifts."

She laughed, a sound reminiscent of silver bells. "I take it you're not a romantic." She turned back to the stove, peeked into the pot, then glanced at the small watch on her bodice. "Only a few more minutes. I hope our guests arrive soon. We're just about ready."

He nodded, but didn't respond. Truth be told, he'd be happy with just the two of them dining on the feast. Working together to prepare the meal in the small kitchen felt comfortable, and the room itself was...homey. When was the last time he'd experienced those emotions?

His gaze bounced around the room. A cream-colored cloth covered the table complementing the yellow earthenware plates and pitchers. Pine boughs and holly branches dotted with bright red berries nestled together in a glass vase. A wide green ribbon was tied around the container. The living room was decorated in shades of blues and greens, bringing to mind the ocean. A pair of intricate cross-stitched samplers hung above the fireplace. Meg was as talented as she was beautiful, and she'd created a warm, inviting place to live. He could see why she had no desire to leave. But surely there was a way for her to have the best of both worlds. If only he could figure out how to make that happen without getting personal.

Legacy of Love

Chapter Twelve

Muffled voices and footsteps sounded from the front porch. Meg sighed and gestured with her wooden spoon toward the door. She would have liked to finish their conversation so she could figure out why he was so adamant about her returning to Boston. Did he have reasons other than the mere desire to complete a mission? "Would you let in our guests?"

Reuben nodded then tromped across the room.

She cocked her head. What was going on in that man's mind?

He opened the door, and the chilly air swept their visitors into the house. He took their coats and hung them on the hooks then led them into the sitting area. Conversation buzzed, punctuated by occasional laughter.

Mrs. Krause smiled and hurried to the kitchen, leaving the others behind. "Smells *gut* in here." She held out a towel-wrapped package. "I'm sure you made dessert, but I brought lebkuchen. They are usually Christmas cookies, but I know they're your favorite." Hesitation lined her face.

"How wonderful. Thank you. They will add a delicious touch to the festivities." Meg gave her a one-armed hug. "Unless they're already on a plate, you can grab one from that cabinet."

The cook smiled and busied herself laying out the treats. "Mr. Jessop seems comfortable acting as host."

Face warm, Meg shrugged. She'd brushed aside the same thought earlier. "Your timing is perfect. Everything is ready. Could you help me set out the food?"

"So, you're avoiding your feelings, ja?"

"It's complicated, Mrs. Krause."

"Love always is." The woman snickered and patted Meg's shoulder before taking the bowl of roasted vegetables to the table. "Come and get it, everyone."

Meg gaped at her then rolled her eyes and turned back to the stove. Her friend had it wrong. There was no love. There couldn't be. She was never leaving Spruce Hill, and he wasn't staying.

Gunny and Harry from the mill sat on either side of Mrs. Krause, and Hal, a logger with Forester Lumber, took a chair across the table. Reuben seated Mrs. Yerburgh, an elderly woman whose husband had passed last Christmas then held the chair for Meg before sitting beside her.

She gazed at the faces surrounding the table, and her heart warmed. The men from the mill and the logger wore faded, but clean, flannel shirts, their beards neatly trimmed, and their hair slicked down. The ladies were dressed in their Sunday-go-to-meeting outfits. Then there was Reuben. He'd spent the last three hours with her preparing the meal, but it seemed as if she were seeing him for the first time. He wore a white cotton shirt, open at the neck, with a charcoal-colored vest that matched his slacks. His jet-black hair was combed back, slightly brushing his collar. His blue eyes sparkled like the ocean on a June day.

As Reuben said the blessing over the meal, she wondered for the umpteenth time if Mr. Pinkerton had sent such a handsome agent on purpose.

The food was distributed, and everyone dug in with gusto. Reuben drew the men into discussions about their work then encouraged the widows to talk about themselves. Meg pressed her lips together as she watched their interaction. He was the perfect host. Why did that thought send shivers down her spine?

Time passed, and the candles burned down. Sunlight faded, and conversation lulled. Empty plates littered the table. Meg rose, and Reuben scrambled to his feet. She gestured for him to remain seated, but he gathered soiled dinnerware and carried it to the sink. She nodded her thanks.

Mrs. Krause cocked her head. "This old woman is tuckered out. Think I'll head home and put up my feet."

"I agree." Mrs. Yerburgh smiled.

"Is that the time—"

"Guess I should get going—"

The men got up and helped older women out of their chairs. In moments, the house was empty save Reuben.

"Well, that was quick. They were here then suddenly gone."

"Seems folks took Mrs. Krause's comments as a cue to leave." He chuckled. "She certainly seems to hold a lot of sway in this town."

"I didn't realize how much until after I went to work for her." Meg scraped the food remains into the trash then ran water into the sink and began to wash the dishes.

Reuben opened several drawers until he found her towels. Standing next to her, he dried the items and put them away.

Homey. Comfortable. Meg shook her head and plunged her hands deeper into the water, scrubbing with a vengeance.

"What did that plate do to you?" Reuben leaned over her shoulder and peeked into the sink.

Her cheeks tingled, and she cringed. "Uh, nothing. Perhaps you should take over. You're the professional."

He tugged a strand of hair that had come loose from her bun and laughed, his breath warm on her ear. "Not a chance."

She resisted the urge to fan her face, mostly because she had a feeling the action would prove useless in cooling herself.

Dishes clinked as he piled them on the shelf. "How about we go for a walk?" He patted his stomach and grinned. "I need to work off some of this lunch."

Perfect. Outdoors, where the air was brisk. "I'd like that." She hurried through the remaining dishes then wiped down the counters. The linens could wait. She turned to survey the rooms to ensure everything else was completed.

Reuben stood at the door, Stetson on his head, holding her cloak. His eyes crinkled in the corners as he smiled. "You've done enough. Time to relax."

She allowed him to wrap the cloak around her, his hands warm on her shoulders. She pulled the hood over her head. With the sun going down, the breeze was sure to hold a nip. They walked outside, and without comment, both turned east which would take them out of town toward the waterfalls. She drew the wool covering closer.

He looked at her with concern. "Are you warm enough?"

"Yes. After the heat of the kitchen, the air feels good out here."

"I think your guests enjoyed themselves. I did. It was great to meet the men from the mill. I met Hal at the mercantile one day shortly after I came. And Mrs. Krause is always a delight."

"She is. I don't know what I'd do without her friendship."

Their feet crunched on fallen maple leaves as they left town and followed the tree-covered path. The tangy scent of red cedar and the huge ponderosa pines enveloped them.

Reuben exhaled a loud breath. "Such a beautiful area of the country. Hard to believe it's taken me this long to get out here."

"You've been a bit busy."

"That I have."

The sound of rushing water filtered through the foliage, and they quickened their pace. A clearing opened up, and the falls thundered in front of them. She glanced at Reuben, whose eyes were wide, and his jaw slack as he took in the power of the water. She'd had the same reaction during her first trip to the spot. "It's overwhelming, isn't it?" She shouted to be heard.

He turned to her, and his face lit up. "Incredible."

She pointed to several large rocks, and they seated themselves, still watching the water cascade into the pool below. "I never tire of seeing this. The seas are vast, and the mountains majestic, but somehow the waterfalls are what speak to me of God's omnipresence."

"I can see why, but I'm having trouble picking a favorite type of scenery. Oregon seems to offer a little bit of every type of God's creation: oceans, lakes, mountains, and valleys. Even a bit of desert and plains."

They sat in silence. Birds flitted overhead, and squirrels leapt between the trees while chipmunks scampered in the undergrowth. The sun dipped below the canopy of leaves, fingers of light filtering through the branches.

"You've done a wonderful job sharing the many facets of your life here. A good job, a cozy home, and a gorgeous area in which to live. Friends who care about you, and a church to feed your soul."

"Yes. I'm truly blessed and have everything I need." Meg sighed. Perhaps he was finally resigned to the fact she would remain, and he'd return to Boston empty-handed.

"But a short trip to your aunt's lawyer, and you could have even more. Yes, your needs are met, but what about your wants? You could live comfortably wherever you wanted to." He pulled up his legs and wrapped his arms around his knees. "You wouldn't have to stay in Massachusetts, but it might be nice to assert your independence there for a while, don't you think?"

"How can you say that?" She frowned. "It's as if you haven't heard a word I've said. You've been here for over two weeks and spent hours with me. How many different ways do I have to show you that money means nothing to me?" Her chest tightened, and she slapped her hand on the surface of the rock. "I don't want the responsibility or the stress that comes from wealth."

He drew back and held up his hands in surrender. "I've been listening, but—"

"But you're just like Tyler and my parents, sure you know what's best for me." Her shoulders drooped. "I thought you were different."

"I am." His eyes shifted, and he studied the ground. "I am different," he repeated.

Was he? He continued to push her to return with him. They'd had the conversation countless times, the same argument over and over. Why was he so adamant? Why did he care so vehemently that she accept the inheritance?

A chill swept over her. Was there something he wasn't telling her?

Legacy of Love

Chapter Thirteen

The cool air nipped at Reuben's cheeks as he strode along Main Street toward the café. Fluffy white clouds drifted overhead, their formations contorting in the robin's-egg-blue sky. The ever-present scent of salt air mingled with the earthy smell of dirt and manure. Dust clouds rose under the horses' hooves as they headed down the street.

During the four days since Thanksgiving, he'd traveled to nearby Astoria to telegraph his report to Mr. Pinkerton and await the man's reply. Succinct to the point of terse, the telegram acknowledged Reuben's efforts, but made it clear success was expected. He tugged at his collar and swallowed. He'd failed Eddie. Would he let down his boss, too? Granted, the mission wasn't life or death this time, but the agency needed to be able to count on him to get the job done.

Upon arrival, he'd checked in with the local sheriff, then walked the beautiful seaside town to collect his thoughts and devise a new strategy to convince Meg of her need to return to Boston. Even if she rejected the inheritance, her family deserved some word from her, didn't they? After wandering the streets and spending hours watching the surf break against the rocks, he'd decided a conversation with her was in order.

With a population of more than six hundred, houses and businesses crowded the streets in contrast to Spruce Hill's sleepy village. Named for the man who'd made a fortune in the fur business then gotten out just as the market was declining, Astoria boasted a vast diversity of architecture. The real-estate mogul would be proud of how far the area had expanded since he'd set up his trading post sixty years ago.

While admiring the double-gabled house of the local tannery owner, Reuben had been regaled by a passerby about how the house had been barged down the river six years ago to its current location without breaking a window or cracking any wallpaper. Apparently, when one had buckets of money, moving a house was of little concern.

He blew out a deep breath, tore off his Stetson, and raked his fingers through his hair before plunking the hat back on his head. He'd arrived in Spruce Hill last night, too late to call on Meg without raising eyebrows. He'd frittered away the morning, waiting until after the lunch rush to head to the café. He pushed open the door, and his gaze roved the room. Vacant. He wended his way through the tables to the kitchen and peeked over the swinging doors. Mrs. Krause was at the counter chopping a pile of carrots. Meg was nowhere to be seen.

"Good afternoon, Mrs. Krause. How are you faring?"

"Gut. I haven't seen you since our lovely meal."

"I had business in Astoria. A pretty town, but it doesn't hold a candle to Spruce Hill."

She nodded. "And your business is complete now?"

"For the time being." He cocked his head. "I'm looking for Meg."

"She's not here. It's her day off."

He slapped his forehead. "Of course. How could I forget? Guess I got my days mixed up."

"Meg told me about your arrangement. You have three weeks remaining until Christmas. Does it really take that long for you to be convinced of her decision?" She narrowed her eyes. "I see you two when you're together. Each one staring at the other when you think no one is paying attention. Is your staying a matter of pride that you might not succeed or because of how you feel?"

"I—"

She held up her hand. "You need to answer that question for yourself, not me. But whatever you decide, do not hurt her." Mrs. Krause's voice was hardened steel, reminding Reuben again of how alike she was with his boss.

"Yes, ma'am." He ducked his head, pivoted on his heel, and hurried from the café. He'd wasted all morning when he could have gone to her home hours ago. He tromped down the street until he arrived at her boarding house. Heart pounding, he raised his hand to knock. Should he have taken time to think about Mrs. Krause's words?

The door swung open, and Meg squealed. She pressed a hand to her chest. "You startled me. I wasn't expecting company." The fading sunlight glinted on her cinnamon-colored hair, and her walnut-brown eyes were wary as they looked at him. Her blue dress peeked out from under her cloak, and she carried a small hat. "Did you need something?"

"Uh...well, I was out of town for a few days and thought we could take a walk now that I've returned. Unless, of course, if you're busy, then we could do it another time." His pulse raced, and he shoved his hands into his pockets as he clamped his lips. He was rambling like a schoolboy.

Her face lit up, and she pinned on her hat, a dark blue confection with ribbons and lace. "You've come just in time. That's exactly what I was planning to do. Did you have somewhere special in mind?"

"Not particularly. With it being midafternoon, we shouldn't go far since darkness falls quickly this time of year." He held out his arm, and she closed the door, then slipped her hand through the crook of his elbow. Her warmth permeated his jacket. Or was that his imagination?

"We can window-shop or head to the gazebo. Your choice."

"I'm not much of a shopper, but if you have errands to run..."

"No. The gazebo, it is."

"Excellent." He guided her toward the far end of town. "You look lovely. Have you had a good day?"

"I've been a layabout, but I have an excuse. I was nearing the end of Miss Alcott's book, and I'm to loan it to Amy when I'm done, so it was important that I finish."

Reuben chuckled. "A good cause if ever I heard one. Listen, I, uh, have a bit of a motive in asking you to walk with me."

Her eyebrow lifted, but she seemed curious rather than suspicious.

"The reason I was away was to send a telegram to Mr. Pinkerton about your refusal of the inheritance and your plans to remain in Oregon." He swallowed. "His response was adamant that I get you on that train."

"Your boss doesn't even know me." Her face darkened. "How can he make that kind of demand?"

He held his hands up in surrender. "He doesn't, but I do, and I've appreciated all that you've done to share Spruce Hill with me. I can see how much you love it, and how immersed in the community you are, but shouldn't I get just as much time to plead my case? Every time I mention going to Boston, you get defensive and close-minded. We agreed to both be open to discussion."

They arrived at the covered pavilion and sat on the bench. She pinked and dipped her head, eyes cast toward the ground. "You're right, and it's only fair to hear your side of things."

"Thank you." He patted her hand. "The pros of staying in Spruce Hill and rejecting the inheritance include your friends, your church, and your job. There seems to be only one con, and that is your lack of money. You've said yourself that you must be frugal to make ends meet. You had friends and a church in Boston that would welcome you back. And gaining the inheritance would solve your financial issues. Mrs. Krause could find anyone to fill your shoes."

She jumped to her feet. "You're as bad as my parents. You wonder why I get defensive with you? In not so many words, you just alluded that my job isn't much and that anyone with half a brain could perform it.

Spruce Hill is not about having an important job or even having enough money to live on. It's the fact that these people have become my family and accepted me in a way my real family never will. Or you."

"But—"

"You will never understand, no matter what I say, and you continue to denigrate me in your efforts to lure me to Massachusetts. Don't wait until Christmas. Leave now."

She stomped down the steps and headed back to town.

"Meg, wait." He started toward her.

She whirled and pointed her finger at him. "Do not follow me. And do not make any more efforts to contact me." She turned and rushed away from him.

Reuben shook his head, and his shoulders sagged as he gaped at her retreating figure. Should he do as she said? No. He'd managed to insult her again. He needed to make things right between them. But how?

Chapter Fourteen

Meg's breath came in gasps as she fled into town, her feet pounding on the hard-packed ground. Tears rolled down her cheeks, and she swiped them away. Perspiration trickled down her spine and stuck stray tendrils of hair to her face. She drew close to the edge of town and slowed her pace as she smoothed her skirts and straightened her shoulders. Dropping her gaze, she wandered along the sidewalk.

Once again, she'd allowed her anger and bitterness to flare at the mere mention of returning to Boston. What was wrong with her? She'd insisted she be allowed to make her case, and as soon as she gave him the same opportunity, she'd lost her temper and run off. Reuben must think her a spoiled and difficult child.

Rather than let him explain his words, she'd made assumptions and inferences that he thought her job meaningless and of little worth. In the blink of an eye, she'd forgotten the hours he spent as a dishwasher, a position that might also be considered to be of no value. Her face heated, and she stopped in her tracks.

Someone ran into her, and she stumbled. A large man, dressed in a well-tailored suit with a crisply ironed light-blue shirt and string tie, glowered at her as he marched past.

"Excuse me, sir."

His response was unintelligible.

She looked around, taking in her surroundings. She'd stopped in front of the mercantile. Should she slip inside in case Reuben came after her? Her lips twisted. Why would he do that? She'd barked at him not to follow her. Being the gentleman he was, he'd heed her words. Her stomach hollowed. She'd made a perfect mess of the entire situation.

"Are you okay, Meg?"

Meg startled and spun.

Amy Powell stood behind her, her sharp gaze searching Meg's face. "You seem to be arguing with yourself, and you nearly got run over. Is there anything I can do for you?"

"I'm not sure anyone can help me." Her face crumpled, and she sagged against the window. "Everything is all jumbled up inside."

"That's understandable. You've had a major upheaval in your life to say nothing of the good-looking man who brought the news. Of those people you know in Spruce Hill, perhaps I can be a voice of reason. After all, I did come from the big city."

"True, but do you have time? You obviously came into town for a reason. It's not like it's a gorgeous summer day, perfect for a stroll."

With a giggle, Amy looped her arm with Meg's and tugged her along the sidewalk. "No, but that's just what we're going to do. Too many eager listeners in any of the shops."

"You're a good friend." Meg sniffled. "I'm not usually such a crybaby."

Amy patted her hand. "Like I said, you've got a lot going on. A girl can only take so much."

Meg nodded and blew out a shuddering breath. "I'm so glad you came by. We haven't talked yet, but I already feel a bit better."

"A burden shared is always lighter." She smiled. "Now, tell me what's gotten you so agitated."

"It's the same old thing. I've got to make a decision about whether or not to return to Boston to claim my inheritance. As you know, I've been showing Reuben around Spruce Hill and involving him in my life in order for him to see that I've no need for the money. I'm not interested in wealth, and I don't want it."

"And that's upsetting?"

"No. I haven't gotten to that part yet. We were at the gazebo just now, and he said I hadn't given him a fair shake to make his case. That I get defensive when it's his turn to present his reasons." Meg's face warmed, and she rubbed her throbbing forehead. "And I just proved his point. The words were barely out of his mouth when I got mad and ran off. That's when you found me."

"Hear me out, okay?" Amy bumped Meg's hip with her own. "Your emotions are scrambled for several reasons, the first of which is obvious. Your aunt meant a great deal to you. You were close before leaving, and now you've lost her. Your grief over her death is fresh and raw. And on top of that, you've got to make a decision in the midst of your sorrow. A decision that involves more emotions...feelings about the place that brought you pain."

Meg's throat thickened. Amy was right. She'd barely had time to absorb the news about Aunt Ida before being forced to determine the course of her future. "When did you get to be so wise?"

"My situation was different, but I, too, faced difficult...life-changing choices." She stopped and turned Meg toward her. "The other reason may be your growing feelings for Reuben. You want him to understand and accept who you are, and it hurts your feelings when you don't think he does. You believe he thinks less of you as a person."

"How—?"

"How can I know exactly what you're going through?" Amy smiled. "I've been where you are. Distraught because I cared and afraid he didn't. Terrified that he might return my feelings. It's an awful place to be in, isn't it?"

"Yes." Meg's voice came out as a whisper. "This is the first time I've ever felt this way about a man." She twisted her fingers. "But with his job sending him all over the country coupled with the possibility he could end up dead, and me living here and unwilling to move, nothing can come of this. Even if he does, you know..."

"Love you?"

"No! No one falls in love in a month. That's preposterous."

"Some people do. Jonathan and I fell in love in less time than that." She cocked her head. "And those who knew us were stunned. On the surface, we're as different as an elephant and a catfish, but inside, where it counts, we hold the same values. He makes me laugh and feel special. I can't imagine my life without him. Set aside the question about your inheritance, and consider how you would have responded if you'd met Reuben on the street...or in the café. Would you have been attracted? Considered accepting an opportunity to be courted by him? Don't allow your past to ruin your future. You'll regret it if you do."

"But a future with Reuben is risky."

"So, you want to hide out in our tiny town and give up the possibility of something special?"

"What if this discussion is a moot point? You claim I have feelings for Reuben, but what about him? He can't possibly be falling for me. He's here to do a job—get me to Boston–that's all, nothing more."

"Have you seen the way the man looks at you? His eyes go soft anytime you're in the vicinity." Amy put her hands on her hips. "He's got it bad and so do you. He's obviously never going to say anything. It's up to you. Sometimes we gals have to take the initiative even if it means rejection."

Meg pulled at her lower lip. Was she willing to risk being spurned? Oh, Aunt Ida, why did you put me in this position?

Chapter Fifteen

The back door opened, and Meg looked up from pouring coffee. Reuben stood on the threshold clutching his Stetson by the brim. A tentative smile hovered on his lips as he dipped his head in greeting. "Mrs. Krause, I thought you might appreciate some help."

Meg's heart skittered. She should be angry that he'd come to the café, but he directed his words to her boss. Was he really only here as a favor to the woman, or was he using the job as an excuse to see Meg?

"Ja. A busy day it's been, and the dishes are stacking high. Thank you for coming."

"Excellent. I'll get right on it." He hung his hat on a hook and slipped behind Meg to walk to the sink.

Her breath hitched at his proximity, and she caught a scent of bay rum. She shouldered her way through the swinging door into the dining room and delivered the sheriff's drink. A quick circulation around the room, and she'd collected three more orders and cleared two tables. Reuben would have his work cut out for him.

She licked her dry lips. How could she be upset at him, yet drawn to him at the same time? Balancing the soiled dishes on her arms, she entered the kitchen and froze. Mrs. Krause was laughing with abandon, and Reuben wore a sloppy grin, all the while up to his elbows in soapy water. She plunked the dishes on the counter next to the sink then went to the stove, all the time ignoring the tall detective. "Two orders of fried chicken, one chicken pot pie."

"Coming right up." Mrs. Krause exchanged a glance with Reuben before she began to work on the food.

Meg narrowed her eyes. What were the two of them up to? She stared at him for a long moment then busied herself getting the customers' drinks. Time passed quickly as she moved back and forth between the dining room and kitchen during the lunch rush. Despite the crowds and fast pace of the meal period, tension drained from her back as Reuben kept her and Mrs. Krause entertained with stories of his exploits, some of which seemed outlandish, so he must be exaggerating his activities for their benefit.

He tugged on her ponytail, then dodged the towel she threw at him, his eyes sparkling with humor. Within thirty minutes of his arrival, he'd managed to clean and stow the tower of dirty dishes, pile of silverware, and collection of pots and pans. After that, he'd kept up with the work, his tanned, muscular arms covered in suds.

Customers trickled out the door, and the dining room was soon vacant. She wiped down the tables and put the chairs in place. Thanks to Reuben's chipper attitude, the meal period had been more fun than usual, and time had flown. He hadn't once mentioned her going to Boston. Was he using a new tactic? Be present, but not talk about the so-called elephant in the room? What would it be like if she said yes and spent a week with him on the train crossing the country? Just the two of them.

Her pulse quickened. He promised to remain with her through the entire process. If she went home, how would Tyler react to his presence? She smirked. Her former fiancé was a fraction of the man Reuben was. But then he would be gone. On to his next assignment. Her shoulders slumped, and she went to the closet and grabbed the broom.

With short, jerking motions, she attacked the debris and dirt. Muffled voices and laughter filtered into the room from the kitchen. She raised her head. What was so funny? Feeling left out, she finished sweeping then went into the kitchen to fill a bucket with water to scrub the wooden floor.

Reuben took the scrap cans outside one at a time while Mrs. Krause cleaned the stove. Meg struggled to lift the bucket, and a pair of strong arms reached around her to latch on to the handle. His firm chest bumped into her back, and her eyes widened. She gripped the sink to keep from swaying.

"You okay?" Concern colored his voice.

Her cheeks heated. "Ah, yes. It's warm in here, don't you think?"

He nodded and carried the bucket into the dining hall.

Mrs. Krause snickered.

Meg whirled. "What?"

"You may as well give up and let yourself fall in love with him."

"That's ridiculous."

"Not from where I stand." She shrugged. "Suit yourself."

Reuben came back into the kitchen. "What else needs to be done?"

"Nothing." Mrs. Krause crossed her arm. "But I have a favor to ask of you."

His face lit up. "Anything."

"I received a telegram from my daughter. She is getting close to delivering her baby, and she has been put on bed rest. Apparently, the doctor has some concerns. She has asked me to come. Would you stay and help Meg run the café? She can cook if you will wait on the customers."

Meg gaped at her boss. "When did you get the message? You've been so calm."

"This morning, and we've been busy, so I didn't have a chance to tell you."

"Of course, you should go. There's a train tomorrow. Will you take it?"

"If you two agree."

Reuben wrapped his arm around Mrs. Krause. "We'll be fine. I'm not as cute as Meg, so the customers might take exception to the plan, but too bad for them." He glanced at Meg. "You're willing to work with me for her, aren't you?"

"Of course." She rushed forward and put her hand on the woman's arm. "We'll take care of everything. You don't need to worry about us."

"I could be gone until after the New Year." She leveled her gaze at Meg. "Should you decide to go to Boston, close the café. Not many people eat out over the Christmas holiday. They'll hardly miss us." Tears filled her eyes. "Thank you. I know this is sudden—"

"Family comes first." Meg sighed.

"And you are family. Don't give it another thought." Reuben glanced at the clock over the door. "I've got a couple of errands to run, but I'll be back to drive the wagon of scrap bins to Mr. Dawson for his pigs. I'll be praying for your daughter and the baby, Mrs. Krause."

"You're a good man."

He bent and kissed her cheek then grabbed his hat and strode from the kitchen.

Meg stared at the space he'd vacated. Mrs. Krause was right. He was a good man. He didn't owe the woman anything, yet he'd agreed to help run the restaurant without a second thought. What would it be like to work side by side with him for the next two weeks? Certainly not dull, but would she be able to remain aloof in the constant presence of his charm?

Chapter Sixteen

Reuben tied the white cotton apron around his waist and grimaced before heading into the café's dining room. Mrs. Krause had been adamant that he look the part when taking over for Meg. At least the infernal thing didn't have a ruffle. He'd have put down his foot if that were the case.

They'd seen the older woman to the stagecoach before dawn, her face wreathed in smiles. Her trunk had weighed as much as a bull steer. How much did one woman need for a month-long trip? Would she really return as she claimed?

He stopped at Sheriff Hobbs's table and poured a mug of coffee. "What'll it be, Ethan?"

"Well, don't you look cute." The sheriff's grin edged toward a smirk. "Never thought I'd see you sashaying around in an apron."

"I'm not sashaying." Reuben leaned toward him. "You ever try to go against Mrs. Krause?"

Hobbs chuckled. "Not on my life. You're a smart man. But in all seriousness, you're doing a nice thing by filling in so she can see her daughter. Above and beyond the call of duty, I'd say."

"I was here anyway. Seemed like the right thing to do." He licked his pencil and held it over his paper. "Meg's made some sort of breakfast casserole. Interested?"

"Got any bacon in it, by chance?"

"Yep."

"Perfect."

Reuben nodded and circulated among the other diners, collecting orders and pouring coffee. He chatted with those he knew and introduced himself to those he didn't. The customers were warm and friendly. If he were to settle down, this is the kind of town where he'd do it.

He clomped back into the kitchen and laid the orders on the counter. "Everyone seems pleased we're keeping things going while Mrs. Krause is away."

Her hair worn in a long braid down her back, Meg stood in front of the stove, a wooden spoon in each hand. Her face was flushed and perspiring, and her eyes wide. "What if I can't keep up with the orders?"

"You'll do fine, and if anyone complains, I'll tell them they need to give us a hand."

"You would?"

"Sure, but these are your friends. No one's going to be ill-tempered." He gestured toward the oven. "Baking the egg dish was a good idea, because it's ready to go. Most of the folks want to try it, so you're off the hook to rustle up a bunch of eggs. How about if I cut the bread and toast it while you prepare the plates?"

She blew out a loud breath, then brushed an errant hair off her forehead with the back of her hand. "Thanks. Just having you in the kitchen makes me feel better."

His chest swelled. He'd felt useless when he'd arrived, but as the morning wore on, they'd developed a system of working together. He hated to see Meg so timid, but he understood her desire to do her job well so as not to let down Mrs. Krause. He uncovered the bread, cut several slices, then put them on a sheet pan and slid them into the oven.

He leaned against the wall and crossed his arms. Keeping one eye on the clock, he watched Meg bustle around the kitchen. With efficient motions, she sliced servings of the casserole, put them on the plates, and piled fried potatoes next to the fluffy egg concoction. He grabbed a towel and nudged her from in front of the stove so he could flip the bread.

Minutes later, he was carrying the steaming food to the customers, feeling ridiculously proud of the lightly browned bread. He rolled his eyes. What would his boss say if he saw him now? He shrugged and moved between the tables to refill coffee. Whatever it took to get the job done.

Returning to the kitchen, he ran water into the sink then added hot water from a pot on the stove before dumping in some soap. He scrubbed at the dishes then rinsed and stacked them to the side. Sweat trickled down his back. Meg had made waiting tables look easy, but the constant walking and smiling was exhausting. He exhaled and rotated his shoulders. Breaking a horse was easier than this.

A wet towel thwapped him on the back, and he looked up.

Meg wore a look of innocence, her eyes wide and a smile on her lips. She held up her hands. "What?"

Laughter bubbled up inside him, and he pretended to throw a handful of water on her.

With a shriek, she covered her face, peeking through her fingers. "You wouldn't dare."

"Only because we've got a dining room full of customers, and I don't want them to hear you cry."

"Ha. You'd be the one crying."

"We'll see about that." He feinted to the left as if to round the island.

She grabbed the pair of wooden spoons and sliced the air with them. "I don't think so." She wielded them like swords, her brow creased in concentration. A bit of flour dusted one cheek.

His fingers itched to wipe away the smudge.

Her smile faltered as he continued to stare, so he winked and picked up a towel to dry his hands. "Playtime is finished. I'd better check on our customers."

"Of course." Her face pinked. "Mrs. Krause would be appalled at our behavior."

"Hardly." He tossed her the towel and pushed through the door. Most of the diners had finished eating, so he cleared plates and gave folks their bills. He pocketed the money and wiped down the tables. Twenty minutes later, the dining room was vacant. Footsteps sounded behind him.

"We did it."

He pivoted. "Did you ever doubt?"

Meg shuffled her feet. "Most of last night."

"Me, too." He stuffed his hands into his pockets. The flour still clung to her cheek.

"Why? My job's easy. Talk to the customers and keep the coffee flowing."

"Easy for you." Reuben frowned. "I delivered the wrong orders twice."

"You'll get the hang of it."

"Nabbing bank robbers is simpler than this."

She giggled and walked to the door where she flipped over the closed sign so they could prepare for lunch.

On her way past him, he reached out and clasped her arm, her skin warm under his touch. His palm tingled. He thumbed the flour from her face. Her eyes widened, pupils dilating, making her brown eyes nearly black. The air sizzled between them as his heart pounded in his chest. She was so close, her lips soft and alluring. What would it be like to kiss them?

Boots clattered on the porch, and he startled. He dropped his hand and blinked. "Uh, you had some flour on your face. Guess I should have told you rather than wipe it off. My manners leave much to be desired."

Her eyes sparkled. "You're a perfect gentleman."

His lungs expanded, and he straightened his spine. Coming from the likes of Meg, the words warmed him. He'd been called a lot of things over the years. Gentleman wasn't one of them.

Legacy of Love

Chapter Seventeen

Flames in the oil lamps reflected in the café windows against the darkness outside. Meg sighed and wiped down the tables while Reuben swept the floor. The days continued to shorten as time marched toward Christmas. Temperatures had hovered in the low forties for the last week, and the skies had been a constant gray. Boston might be cold and snowy during the winter months, but blues skies with fluffy, white clouds were the norm.

She finished the tables and went into the kitchen to retrieve the cashbox so she could close out the day's earnings. Setting it on the counter, she opened the lid of the wooden cigar box, and the pungent smell of tobacco wafted toward her. Bills and coins mingled with orders. She separated and stacked the orders then sorted the money by denomination. Her lips moved as she counted. Math had never been her best subject, so she took her time to ensure accuracy.

Behind her the doors swung open, and Reuben's distinctive rolling gait sounded behind her. He went to the stove and poured the last of the coffee into two mugs and set one near her elbow. She smiled and lifted the fragrant brew to her lips. "Thank you. I'm almost done here, then we can sit and chat if you'd like, or head home if you're tired."

He leaned against the wall and cradled his mug with both hands. "I'm in no hurry. Nothing to do once I get back to the boarding house except stare at the walls."

"So, I'm an acceptable alternative to boredom?"

His face reddened. "No, I mean—"

"I'm kidding." She set down the coffee. "I won't be much longer." Aware of his gaze, she tried to concentrate on her work, but after the sum came up different three times, she blew out a deep breath. "How about if you wait in the dining room?"

"Guess you don't need my *supervision.*" He chuckled and slipped from the room.

She watched the doors swing back and forth until they finally settled to a close. Three days had passed since Mrs. Krause left them in charge, and they'd fallen into a routine. Reuben had learned the tasks quickly and become adept at juggling the myriad tasks associated with waiting on customers. She'd been embarrassed to discover his coffee was better than hers, so he now arrived early enough to have it ready before breakfast. His dry sense of humor and constant teasing kept her from taking herself too seriously, finally allowing her to shed her worry that she might mess things up for the kind woman who'd taken her in five years ago.

Reuben assured her that Mrs. Krause wouldn't have left them to work the café if she thought they'd fail. His deep-blue eyes seemed to caress her face as he talked, but she must be imagining the emotion. He had an important career: rounding up bandits, robbers, and gangs, and ensuring the safety of the public. She was a simple waitress. She'd accused him of demeaning her position, but in truth, she often agreed with the assessment. The townspeople were warm and friendly toward her, but they'd be that way to anyone who held the job.

Finally finished tallying the day's take, she bagged the money in preparation for taking it to the bank in the morning then stuffed the receipts into a large envelope for Mrs. Krause. All three mealtimes had been packed with customers, unusual for mid-December. Perhaps the novelty of a broad-shouldered, handsome waiter had brought in extra patrons. She shook her head. That wouldn't account for all the men who'd stopped in.

She patted her hair. A mirror would be out of place in the kitchen, but it would be nice to know whether she looked a total fright or not. Meg rubbed her hands on her skirts then grabbed her coffee and slipped into the dining room. Reuben sat in a chair tilted against the wall, his chin on his chest and his eyes closed. His breathing was deep and even. Laugh lines bracketed his eyes, but the rest of his face was smooth, at peace.

Would he be flustered to awaken and find her staring at him? She tiptoed back into the kitchen then clomped her heels as she reentered the dining room. The noise had served its purpose, and he sat up, coffee mug in hand. How could his eyes glitter with clarity after being asleep seconds ago? She took hours to shake the bleariness each morning.

"Mrs. Krause will be pleased with how well the café is doing in her absence." Meg pulled out a chair with her foot and sat. "I believe we're getting the hang of things."

"I never had any doubts." He smiled and sipped his drink. "It feels good to have tasks completed at the end of each day, to see results. When I'm hunting down criminals, it can be weeks before I make any progress."

"That would be frustrating for me."

He rubbed at the rim of the mug. "Some guys find it's not for them either. Their first case tells them whether they're going to like the job. Folks assume being an agent is exciting, but in reality, good detective work mostly involves tedious tasks like questioning witnesses, following up on leads, poring over lists, and covertly watching suspects. We do everything we can to avoid chases and shoot-outs."

"Making the job less dangerous."

"In some ways, but there's always the chance of the best plans going awry." A shadow passed over his face. "Fortunately, those times don't occur often."

She knew he was thinking about his friend, Eddie. "But they're difficult when they do happen."

He met her gaze, and his eyes softened. "But good friends and time help." He drained his mug and grimaced. "Probably not the best pot of coffee I've ever made."

"It's later than you think. That brew has been sitting on the stove for hours."

With a yawn, he stretched his arms over his head. "I'm bushed, and you must be as well. Let's head out."

Meg looked away from his lithe form, her heart pounding. She had to get a grip if she was going to survive the next few weeks. She climbed to her feet, picked up her mug and his to have something to do with her hands, and carried them into the kitchen. She set them in the sink and fanned her face. Good thing the temperature outside was chilly for her walk home. She pulled her cloak from the hook and wrapped it around her shoulders.

Reuben came into the kitchen, plunked his Stetson on his head, and slipped into his leather coat. He held the door for her, and they stepped outside.

She stumbled on the uneven planks of the porch and lost her balance. Before she could fall, he'd caught her in his arms. Pressed against him, she could feel his heart beating in rhythm to her own. Her eyes widened. A fingernail moon hung in the black expanse, so she struggled to see his face in the murky night, but she felt his closeness when his breath stroked her cheek. A shiver wriggled up her spine.

Was he going to kiss her? Did she want him to?

His lips brushed hers then pressed more firmly, and her stomach fluttered. Was this what it felt like to be in love?

Chapter Eighteen

Heart thudding in his chest, Reuben raised his head and squinted at Meg's face. Her eyes drifted open, clouded for a moment then cleared. The corners of her mouth curved up, and her cheeks were flushed. What was going through her mind?

His lips were still warm from hers, and she fit in his arms perfectly. Working side by side to ensure success for Mrs. Krause had bonded them into partners, but more than that, their time together had been sweet, filling him with contentment. He went to bed each night remembering moments that had occurred during the day. When he'd awaken, he would jump out of bed in anticipation of seeing her. He sought her opinion in everything, appreciating her quick assessment of a situation and ability to devise a creative solution, no matter how insignificant the decision.

Certainly, her external beauty attracted him, but it was her essence that captured his heart—her stalwart faith, quick wit, tenacity, and desire to help others. A vision of her seated on the ground next to the little boy at the orphanage floated through his mind. The joy spilling from her eyes when he hugged her. The laughter that bubbled up from inside her as the two played in the dirt. He'd never met anyone like her.

She'd make a wonderful mother someday. Why hadn't one of the young men in Spruce Hill already claimed her? Had they tried and been spurned? Had her experience with her parents' attempt to arrange a marriage put her off from ever desiring a husband and children?

Her smile wavered, and a sheen of moisture filled her eyes.

He dropped his arms and stuffed his hands into his pockets. She was obviously regretting their kiss. Clearing his throat, he winced. "I'm sorry. I was...uh...that was uncalled for...I didn't mean—"

Meg put her hand on his arm, her fingers trembling against his sleeve. "I'm enjoying our friendship, Reuben, but there can be nothing more than that. We're here to do a job for Mrs. Krause, and when it's over, you'll return to Chicago or head to wherever Mr. Pinkerton sends you next, and I'll remain in Spruce Hill. We need to maintain a professional distance until you're gone."

His stomach twisted. Surely, she felt drawn to him. She'd responded to him. Not at first, but then her lips had given way, and she'd returned his kiss. The nearly moonless night failed to illuminate her face. All he could do was listen to her voice, and it was filled with an emotion he couldn't place. Regret? Sorrow? Disappointment?

He scrubbed at his face and blew out a deep breath as his shoulders slumped. She wasn't saying anything he didn't already know. His departure loomed, but he'd been pushing it to the back of his mind in the hope that she would change her decision and accompany him to Boston. She'd been completely honest about her lack of desire for wealth from the moment he'd arrived. He straightened his spine and nodded even though she couldn't see him in the total darkness. "I'm sorry. Of course, you're right. Thank you for not allowing my indiscretion to ruin our friendship." His lips felt wooden as the words tumbled out.

"I need to get home. Will you walk me the rest of the way, or would you prefer to bow out?" This time her voice held concern.

"I'd like to accompany you. Spruce Hill may be small, but there is still opportunity for misdeeds."

"Always the Pinkerton agent." Humor laced her words.

"Probably until the day I die even after I no longer work for them."

"I'm glad. I feel safe when you're with me."

Sliding her hand into the crook of his elbow, he led her down the sidewalk as he swallowed a sigh. Was safety all she felt?

Her skirts rustled in the silence.

Somewhere in the distance a coyote howled. Then another barked in response. Better to keep his mouth shut and let the wildlife do the talking. He'd said and done enough already.

They arrived at her boarding house, and he waited while she dug her keys from the small reticule that hung from her wrist by a drawstring. Metal sounded against metal as she fumbled to unlock the door. Should he offer to ensure no one was in the house? No. That would be assuming too much on his part.

She opened the door and turned toward him. "Thanks for all your hard work today. I'll see you in the morning."

"That you will. Have a good night, Meg."

The door closed with a thud, and he hovered outside. Seconds later, a match flared through the gauzy curtains and illuminated her profile as she put the flame to the wick then set the chimney in place. He waited a few more minutes, then shrugged and headed toward the hotel where he was staying. Why did he always look for danger?

Spruce Hill wouldn't attract the kind of nefarious outlaws he'd tracked over the years. The tiny village watched out for its own. The sheriff had made that clear when he checked on Reuben's credentials. He had no doubt the man considered restraining him until the report came back. He'd have done the same thing if he wore the shiny tin star. He grinned then sobered as Meg's words came crashing back into his head.

She'd made it clear there was nothing for him here once Mrs. Krause returned. Meg wasn't going to Boston, no matter how many outings they took or how many different ways he tried to convince her otherwise. Unfortunately, he'd grown to love the small haven in the few short weeks he'd lived here, but the town wasn't large enough to need two lawmen, and the last thing they needed was a Pinkerton agent.

He raked his fingers through his hair. Why did life have to be so complicated?

Chapter Nineteen

Meg wiped perspiration from her forehead with her sleeve. Despite the winter temperatures outside, the kitchen was hot and humid as usual. Steam rose from the pot of potatoes boiling on top of the stove, and heat emanated from the oven where a pork shoulder was roasting. Her damp dress clung to her back. The lunch rush was over, and she was nearly finished preparing for dinner. With any luck, she'd have an hour or so to put up her feet before the first diners wandered in.

She cast a sidelong glance at Reuben who stood at the sink washing dishes. Two days had passed since their kiss, but she couldn't seem to purge it from her mind. As promised, his behavior was professional, never once referring to the incident. He was solicitous and kind, but no longer teased her by tugging on her hair or making jokes about something she did or said.

Her shoulders slumped. Wasn't there some way to go back to their warm friendship without worrying about romantic entanglements?

"Hey, I'm finished here. I was going to take the slop to Mr. Dawson and dump the trash, but do you have something else that needs to be done first?" He dried his hands on a towel, then hung the cloth on a hook. His eyes were clear and warm, but no longer held the twinkle she'd come to know. "I've already wiped down the tables and swept the floor in the dining room."

"Goodness, you've done a lot. The potatoes are almost done, and I was going to shell the peas and make gravy. You're free until five o'clock."

"Isn't that a little late?"

"No, folks don't usually start coming in until then. We should be fine."

"Okay. See you later." He grabbed his hat and coat and slipped outside without a backward glance.

Meg stared at the door for a long moment. What was wrong with her? She'd asked him to act less personal, and now that he was, she didn't like it. How could life turn upside down in a few short weeks?

A shadow appeared in the window, and she brightened. She smoothed her apron and pinned a smile on her face. A knock sounded, and she went to the door. "You don't need to—oh, Amy, it's you."

"Gee, that's a lively welcome. I take it you were expecting someone else." She hugged Meg. "Perhaps your handsome helper."

Meg shook her head. A lie she'd ask forgiveness for later. "It's wonderful to see you. What brings you into town?"

"The supplies Jonathan ordered arrived, and I couldn't come without stopping by."

"Can I get you something to eat? I could make you a sandwich."

"No, we packed a picnic for the return trip."

"Sounds romantic."

Amy blushed and nodded. "We try to take time once a week to do something special even if it's just a meal by the roadside on the way home."

"At least let me get you some cookies. I baked them this morning."

"I love your desserts." She sniffed the air. "Oatmeal?"

"You've got a good sense of smell." Meg laughed and handed Amy a cookie then wrapped a half-dozen more in a towel. "Do you have time for a chat? You can help me shell the peas."

Amy crossed her arms and leaned against the wall. "Absolutely. Jonathan said he'd be at least thirty minutes, but hopefully he'll be longer."

"It will be cooler in the dining room. Grab the pods, and I'll get us a couple of bowls."

Minutes later they were ensconced at a table, the sound of the tiny orbs rattling in the bowl.

"Is everything all right, Meg? I mean, I know running the café is a lot to handle, and you may not have made your decision about the bequest yet, but you seem discouraged."

"I didn't think anyone would notice."

"Most people wouldn't, but I can read you pretty well by now."

Meg shelled several pods then looked up at her friend. "I think I've made a mess of things. Reuben and I have been getting along, and the café is running smoothly. We've gotten to know each other. A couple of nights ago he kissed me."

Amy shot up in the chair. "I knew you two should be together. When you came out to the house, I could see your affection."

"But that's just it. We're not *together*. I told him there can never be anything between us. He's leaving. I'm staying."

"You didn't."

"I did, and he's been nothing but polite ever since." Tears pricked the backs of her eyes. "I hate to admit it, but I'll miss him."

"Oh, Meg. Of course, you will. You care for him. Why are you going to let him go without telling him?"

"Because he might not feel the same way. Maybe he's just interested in me for the money."

"Then you've decided to accept the inheritance?" Amy cocked her head.

"No."

"Then his feelings are definitely not about the money." She patted Meg's knee. "I see how he looks at you. He's got it bad. And I think you do, too. And if neither one of you tells the other, you'll both squander a God-given opportunity of love."

"You think God sent him?"

"I don't know." Amy shrugged. "But I do believe God will put up roadblocks if your relationship shouldn't proceed."

"Isn't Reuben getting on a train in two weeks a roadblock?"

"Only if you let it be."

"What if he's no different than Tyler?"

Amy scoffed, "From what you've told me about that man, Reuben is nothing like him, and anything good is worth the risk, especially love."

Reuben's head appeared above the kitchen door, and he waved.

A chill swept over Meg. How much of the conversation had he heard?

Legacy of Love

Chapter Twenty

The sound of the piano faded away, and Meg blew out a sigh. Today's music and message had been a comforting balm. She'd let the stress of operating the café, the worry about her decision, and grief of her aunt's death overtake her focus on God and His plans for her. As usual, she was running ahead then beckoning for Him to catch up. Trying to figure out things on her own. No wonder she was exhausted.

Forgive me, Father. I want Your best for me, so help me know what You would have me to do. Thank You for the chance to help Mrs. Krause so she can be with her daughter. And thank You for this church and this town that have enveloped me with their embrace, never once making me feel like an outsider.

Pastor Kearns intoned the benediction. Meg rose with the rest of the congregation who gathered their belongings then shuffled into the small room off the sanctuary that served as a fellowship hall. On the plank table, dozens of steaming dishes gave off fragrant aromas. Her stomach rumbled in anticipation. How lovely to eat food someone else had cooked.

Time continued to gallop past. Next Sunday was Christmas Eve. She'd received several invitations for Christmas Day, but none had struck a chord with her, so she'd probably spend the day in solitude. Two days off in a row would be delightful, giving her body a rest from hunching over the stove all day. She'd never realized how wearing it could be to stand in one place for hours on end. Her feet ached by closing time when she waitressed, but her back and shoulders were never as tight as now. How did Mrs. Krause do it at her age?

Meg wended her way through the crowd toward two women who were laying out utensils, plates, and napkins. "Do you ladies need any help?"

Mrs. Lovell, a plump, gray-haired lady who was eighty, if she was a day, smiled and shook her head. "No, dearie. We're fine. You go talk to the other young people."

"Are you sure? I could fill the pitchers."

"You provide hospitality all week. Let us serve you."

"Thank you. That's very kind." She turned and hesitated, at a loss about which of the other *young people* to chat with. Most of her friends were married, so the idea of being a third wheel in a conversation was repugnant.

She caught sight of Reuben in the far corner with four small children, perhaps four- or five-year-olds. He was seated on the floor cross-legged, with a towheaded boy on his lap while the others clustered around them. A broad smile lit up his face as he spoke, and his eyes twinkled, even from this distance. He poked the belly of one of the little girls, and she giggled. He tousled her hair then dipped his head and murmured to the child on his legs. He'd make a wonderful father someday. Did he want children? They'd never ventured onto that topic.

Her heart squeezed. Why should they talk about a family? She'd continued to protest that their relationship couldn't be anything more than friendship. And yet when she thought about his leaving without her, a bitter taste settled in her mouth. Meg shook her head and grimaced. She was acting like a twelve-year-old schoolgirl with a crush.

No. Her feelings seemed to be much more.

His mere presence brightened her days. Each morning she anticipated the sound of his tread entering the café. His voice as they worked side by side providing meals for the community. His warmth when he squeezed past her in the kitchen's tight quarters, his scent tickling her senses. And she still couldn't get their kiss off her mind.

"He's good with them, isn't he?"

Meg startled and whirled.

Sheriff Hobbs stood at her elbow. "Do you have a few minutes?"

"Sure." What could he want? Had he unearthed more information about Reuben? The sheriff wasn't one for idle conversation, so he must have something to say.

They sauntered out of earshot of the throng, and she looked at him with anticipation. "Something on your mind, Sheriff Hobbs?"

Hands stuffed in his pockets, he rocked back on his heels. "You know I'm not a man to get involved in the personal lives of the townsfolk, but I'm concerned about you. You've always been slender, but you've lost weight." His cheeks reddened. "Have you been to see the doc?"

"Nothing wrong with my health." She frowned. "Just a lot on my mind, and working extra hours to make sure the café runs smoothly for Mrs. Krause. And to be honest, hanging over a stove all day fiddling with food does a number on my appetite."

"Fair enough. But I hope you'll consider some free advice. Like I said, it's not my nature to butt in; however, I've learned a few things over the years, and one of them is that home is a state of mind. I know you've been happy here. You'd hit a rough patch before you came to us, and we helped steer you through your woes. And you've become a big part of our community. I know the Quinns appreciate all you do at the orphanage."

He rubbed his jaw. "It'd be a shame for you to lose out on a chance at happiness because of stubbornness. You know if you had to leave, you'd be welcome back anytime. Anyway, I just wanted to tell you that." He looked uncomfortable as he patted her shoulder then walked away.

She gaped at his retreating back. She'd be offended at his meddling if he hadn't been so sincere. In the five years since she'd been living in the town, that was the longest conversation they'd ever had.

"Honey, can you grab the hymnals? We're going to do a bit of a songfest after lunch is over." Mrs. Broomfield, the church pianist nudged Meg's shoulder.

"Yes, ma'am." Meg forced a smile. "Where would you like me to put them?"

The middle-aged woman gestured to a nearby windowsill. "How about over there?"

"Certainly." Meg hurried back to the sanctuary to collect the music books. Voices sounded, and she froze in the doorway.

"I don't know what to do, Pastor. I've fallen in love with her, but I'm hesitant to tell her. She needs to return to Boston and claim the inheritance for her own good. Can you help me convince her to go?"

Meg's hand flew to her mouth as her head tried to process what she'd heard. The voice belonged to Reuben. Surely, he didn't love her. He was just saying that to get the pastor to agree with him. How could she have trusted someone so underhanded?

Legacy of Love

Chapter Twenty-One

The café was jammed with patrons. Conversation was punctuated with laughter as silverware clinked on china and chairs scraped the floor. Reuben threaded his way between the tables, a stack of plates on his arms. He reached his destination and deftly delivered the meals to the six men seated at the far table. They nodded their thanks and dug in as soon as the food hit the surface. Each one of the men wore a faded cotton shirt and buckskin pants, with a long beard and hair that straggled past his shoulders. A reminder had been necessary for them to remove their hats when they'd arrived, to which they'd complied with sardonic smirks. Who were these guys?

"More coffee, gentlemen?" He pinned on a smile, but none of them looked up, merely shaking their heads as they continued to fork food into their mouths. The acrid smell of alcohol hovered above them. They didn't appear drunk, but apparently had imbibed enough liquor to reek of the stuff.

He moved to the next table then the next until he'd checked on all the customers. Maybe he'd been a lawman too long, but his senses told him he needed to keep an eye on the men. With the exception of the six cowboys, he knew or at least recognized the rest of the patrons, upstanding and polite citizens of Spruce Hill and nearby Astoria.

His back stiff and unyielding, he strode into the kitchen. He grabbed a mug and poured himself some coffee then leaned against the wall while Meg busied herself at the stove. Face flushed in the heat, errant strands of hair stuck to the sides of her face. The bun at the base of her head that had been smooth and pristine prior to breakfast, now hung askew. Even with her disheveled appearance, she was beautiful.

She glanced in his direction, one eyebrow quirked, and her lips set in a slash. "Something eating you?"

"Is it that obvious?"

"Let's just say I hope you weren't wearing that expression in the dining room. That's not the atmosphere we're aiming for here."

Sipping the hot, smoky liquid, he gazed at her over the rim. She'd been short with him since he'd arrived. Did she think she was the reason for his foul mood? Or was she still upset about the kiss? He never should have given in to the temptation, but her lips had been so close, so alluring.

This mission was supposed to be easy. Get in, get the girl, get out. So far, easy had yet to enter the picture. Of course, he had himself to blame. Falling in love with her had added all sorts of complications. Maybe a different line of work was in order. He could be a cowboy like the guys out front. Just men and horses, no women. That sort of job had to be more peaceful. Certainly, less perplexing.

He set down the coffee and jerked his head toward the dining room. "We've got a group of strangers who are a bit less genteel than I'd like."

"We're not exactly Boston's Parker House." Anger laced her words. "What did you expect?"

His chest tightened, and he blew out a breath. "Basic manners, but these seem to be out of reach for these particular *gentlemen.* They've got an edge to them. I can't put my finger on it, but I don't trust them."

Her eyes widened, and her hand clenched the wooden spoon. "Should we get Sheriff Hobbs in here? Do you think they're bandits? Should I take the till to the bank?"

"No, but I'll be glad when they leave." He drained his coffee and put the mug in the sink.

Raucous laughter filtered into the kitchen, then the sound of a chair hitting the floor. He held up his hand, palm out toward Meg. "Stay here. Things are about to get interesting." He pushed through the batwing doors into the dining room. All but three tables had been vacated. He strode toward the six men. Wait. There were now only five. His eyes narrowed. Where had the sixth man gone?

He forced a smile and loosened his joints to appear jocular. "Hey, boys, sounds like you're having the time of your lives. Enjoying your food?" He stood inches behind the man he'd earlier determined was the ringleader. If he was the instigator, he'd have to push Reuben down to get out of his chair. He studied each of the men. In the short span of time since he'd served them, their eyes had become clouded and unfocused, and the smell of alcohol hung over the table like a cloud.

The ringleader twisted his neck and glared at Reuben. "Just having a bit of fun. Any law against that?" His words were slurred.

"Fun, no. Public drunkenness, yes."

"We're not drunk." The man's face darkened.

"Perhaps not, but you're mighty close. I suggest you boys head on out." He gestured to the empty plates. "It appears you've finished your meal."

"We haven't had our dessert yet." The smallest of the men frowned, his voice whiny.

Reuben crossed his arms and rocked on his heels. "I'm afraid we're all out. Seems one of your friends has already gone. If you join him right now, your lunch is on the house. How's that for a deal?"

"Join him?" Another man cackled. "I wouldn't mind that."

"Then it's settled." Reuben stepped back so the leader could rise from the table. "I hope you boys have a good rest of your day."

A scream split the air.

Meg!

In a flash, Reuben pulled his pistol from his ankle holster and raced into the kitchen. The missing cowboy had pushed Meg against the wall, his hands gripping her shoulders and trying in vain to land a kiss. Her head jerked back and forth stymying his efforts. One hand pointing the gun at her assailant, Reuben used the other to grab the back of the man's shirt and yank him away. "Get your hands off her."

The man grunted in surprise then swung a meaty fist at Reuben, but only struck air.

Reuben pressed the gun's muzzle into the goon's side.

Her face white and wet with tears, Meg wrapped her arms around her middle. "He—"

"I know. You're okay now. He's one of the *guests* I was concerned about. I'm going to march all of them down to the sheriff's office. Lock this door then the front door after I leave."

She nodded and swiped at the moisture on her cheeks. "Thank you." She drew in a shuddering breath. "If you weren't here... Thank you for saving me."

His chest swelled. He'd like to spend a lifetime keeping her safe. "I'll be back as soon as I can. Don't open the doors for anyone but me."

"Okay."

He poked the man with the gun and pointed toward the dining room. "After you."

With a grumble, Meg's attacker shoved his way through the door then stopped. "Looks like they got the bead on you. They're gone."

"More importantly, they've left you holding the bag. Some kinds of friends you got there. Now, get doing. We've got an appointment with the sheriff."

Chapter Twenty-Two

Little noise filtered from the dining room into the café's kitchen as Meg glanced at the clock above the door. Another hour until lunch was over. They'd served only five parties since opening for the meal. Breakfast had been somewhat busy, but not as hectic as usual. With Christmas only three days away, customers were at home with visiting families or out of town. Being open hardly seemed worth it, but what else would she do if not work?

Reuben's laugh sounded, and she smiled. He'd been such a help while Mrs. Krause was visiting her daughter. They'd received a telegram with the news a healthy baby boy had been delivered, and that they were welcome to close the restaurant starting on Christmas Eve. Mrs. Krause would reopen around the fifth or sixth of January.

Meg blew out a deep breath. Once they weren't working the café, he could head home, and her life would go back to normal. Such as it was. Without his teasing presence, things would be very quiet. Boring. Empty. She stared out the window. Swollen black clouds hung in the gray sky. How long before the deluge that would turn the street to a muddy quagmire?

The door hinges squeaked, and footsteps clomped into the kitchen behind her. She glanced over her shoulder. Reuben was at the stove pouring coffee into a pair of mugs. With a grin he winked at her then ducked into the dining room.

Her heart thudded, and her stomach buzzed as if a hummingbird was trapped inside. She pressed her hand against her middle. She didn't want her life to go back the way it was. She'd been content, but life was not nearly as rich as it was now that Reuben was part of each day.

His warmth, sense of humor, and teasing, but mostly his integrity and faith had touched her in unexpected ways. She sought to be a better woman. He'd treated her with respect and friendliness despite the number of times she'd lost her temper and pushed against his advice to claim Aunt Ida's bequest.

What would her aunt tell her to do?

Memories of their outings washed over her. Sitting in a wagon headed to some destination, his firm arm and shoulder pressed against hers, providing safety and security. Nestled under a tree on a picnic blanket, his ice-blue eyes snapping with intelligence and wit. On the pew at church worshiping together, his bass voice rumbling in his chest as he sang the hymns. The muscles in his back straining against his shirt as he bent over the sink washing stacks of dishes, carrying the trash bins outside, or moving tables to clean the floor.

He was like no man she'd ever met. Attacking every task, no matter how mundane, with a sense of adventure. He'd never once complained about the chores. What man is happy doing so-called women's work? Especially a man trained in soldiering and law.

Oh, Lord, what am I going to do? I can no longer ignore the fact that I've fallen in love with Reuben. He is everything a woman could hope for in a husband, yet there's no way we can marry. He'll be leaving in two days' time, and I'll be alone.

Her chin trembled, and she caught her lower lip between her teeth. Since when was she a crybaby? Instead of mourning his absence, she should reminisce about the good times. She grabbed a cloth and soaked it with water then scrubbed the counters. Standing around moping wasn't doing her any good nor was the work getting done.

She finished with the counters and turned her attention to the stove. At this point it was unlikely that she would be making any more meals. Perspiration trickled between her shoulder blades and formed at her hairline as she scoured grease and remnants of food from the metal surface.

"What did that stove do to you?" Reuben chuckled as he scraped the soiled plates then put them in the sink.

"I was getting antsy." Meg tossed the dirty cloth into the bucket and sighed. She must look a fright. Her face heated. There was nothing she could do about her appearance now, and he'd seen her look this way for weeks. But today it mattered. Today, she wanted to look her best. "Any more orders?"

He shook his head. "No, in fact everyone's gone. The place is empty. There's only fifteen minutes left for service. How about if we close? I doubt Mrs. Krause would mind."

"If you think it's okay." She shrugged. Since when was she indecisive? Ugh. "Yes, let's close." She pushed past him into the dining room and went to the door. She flipped the sign and locked the knob.

A young man dressed in a rumpled suit waved at her through the glass, and her heart fell. She was in no mood to cook for anyone else. She pinned on a smile and opened the door.

He held up a large, slim envelope. "Miss Underwood?"

"Yes, that's me."

"Letter for you." He handed her what looked like a receipt. "Please sign on the bottom line attesting you've taken possession of the document."

Her eyes widened. "Uh, okay." She laid the paper on the closest table and took the proffered pen. Hands slick, she scribbled her signature as requested and returned the instrument and receipt. "Just a minute." She turned to go to the kitchen for her reticule, but Reuben stood behind her.

"I've got this." He dug into his pocket then pressed a coin into the messenger's hand.

"Thank you, sir." The young man slipped out the door.

Meg stared at the envelope, her mouth dry. The name and address of a Boston law firm was in the upper right hand corner. "What do you think is inside?"

Reuben's brow creased. "Perhaps something connected to your aunt's estate."

"Of course." Fingers trembling, she tore open the flap and withdrew two sheets of paper. She scanned the words, and nausea threatened to overwhelm her. A lump formed in her throat, and her breath hitched.

"Are you all right? You look like you've seen a ghost." Reuben squeezed her shoulder.

"I have." She shoved the papers into his hands and dropped into a chair then hunched into herself. *Dear God, this couldn't possibly be in Your plans, could it?*

"You're being sued?"

"It looks that way. If I understand what I read, Tyler is claiming I broke our contract of an arranged marriage, and as such he's sustained damages, especially to his reputation. I'm to be held culpable, but if I agree to marry him, the charges will be dropped." Her voice broke. "What am I going to do?"

Chapter Twenty-Three

Reuben's heart jumped into his throat, and he raked his fingers through his hair. Who did this Tyler guy think he was? Bullying a woman into marrying him. What kind of man pulled that kind of stunt? He stilled. A man motivated by greed. The money and value of the house Meg stood to inherit was significant. Word was apparently out among Boston's elite, and her ex-fiancé was the first of many sharks circling in hope of securing her vast wealth. Little did the man know that she had no intentions of accepting the bequest.

He grimaced and knelt in front of Meg. She'd laced her fingers together in her lap, and her knuckles were white. He cradled her fists in one palm, his thumb stroking the back of her hand, and with the other he lifted her chin until her gaze met his. Her face was ashen, and a sheen of moisture covered her eyes. His stomach dropped at her bereft expression.

"What am I going to do?" she repeated.

"First, let's pray and ask for God's guidance. Then we'll figure out the best way to proceed. How's that sound?"

She nodded, her chin trembling.

Head bowed, he inhaled a deep breath then blew it out. "Father God, we're desperate. This letter has come out of the blue and shocked us. We don't understand the legal ramifications and what is required of Meg, but You do. We need Your help. Please work this out for Meg's good and Your glory. I don't want to be selfish, Father, but I'd rather she didn't have to marry this man. Can You please arrange it so she doesn't have to if she doesn't want? Thank You for Your wisdom and strength in this situation. Help us not to panic. It sure is tempting to do so. We ask all these things in the name of Your Son Jesus, amen."

He opened his eyes and raised his head. Tears had tumbled down Meg's cheeks, and he pulled out his handkerchief from his back pocket and dabbed at the wetness. "I will be beside you the whole time. Okay? I need you to answer one question, then I'll know how to proceed."

"All right." She sniffled.

"Do you want to marry Tyler?"

"No!" She reared up in the chair, her eyes wide. "Not in the least. Why would you ask that?"

"Because in my line of work we don't assume anything. I didn't think you did, but I had to be sure." He smiled and patted her hands still clutching his hanky. "And I'll ensure you don't have to. The agency has far-reaching resources. They can access information that we can't. However, I need to warn you that you may have to return to Boston to fight this. I only know the laws that apply to chasing bandits and bank robbers, so I'm not sure if your presence will be required in court, if it gets that far."

Meg took a shuddering breath. "Thank you for helping me." Her voice was barely above a whisper. "I'm still nervous, but praying helped, and I don't feel alone anymore."

His chest swelled. "You're not alone. Now, I'm going to send a couple of cables: one to the attorneys so they know we've received the documentation and one to the agency so they can get started. I'm also going to notify Sheriff Hobbs, so he won't be blindsided if something, or someone, shows up."

Her hand flew to her mouth. "You don't think Tyler would come here, do you?"

"Not again, but I want to ensure we're prepared, and the sheriff may think of things we wouldn't. Do you want to come with me or remain at the café? Either one is fine with me."

"I need to finishing cleaning up, and the work might help take my mind off this."

"All right. I'll be back as soon as I can." He climbed to his feet then bent and pressed a kiss on her forehead. He fought the urge to pull her into his arms as a way to drive away the fear he read in her eyes. Instead, he would use every ounce of his strength to fix this problem for her. He stroked her jaw with his forefinger then turned and strode out the door.

His boots clomped on the wooden sidewalk as he marched to the general store where the telegraph office resided. He hated to have Meg's business known in town, but a trip to Astoria would take too much time. He'd have to rely on the shopkeeper's discretion.

A bell jangled above the door as he entered the shop. Hank Densley looked up from behind the counter and nodded a greeting. "Good day to you, Mr. Jessop. What can I do for you?"

"I need to send a couple of telegrams of a sensitive nature." He narrowed his eyes at the shopkeeper. "Is that something you're able to do?"

The man straightened his spine and met Reuben's steely gaze with one of his own. "Absolutely. Rest assured the contents of your telegrams will remain confidential."

Tension slid from Reuben's shoulders, and he smiled. "Excellent." Moments later, he finished writing out the missives and paid Mr. Densely. "I'll be back for my confirmation shortly." He might just pick up something nice for Meg during his return visit.

"Yes, sir."

First errand complete. Now to the sheriff's office. He pressed his lips together. The agency had lots of investigators, some of the best in the country, but did Mr. Pinkerton have access to attorneys who could untangle this mess? He froze. Did their opponent have enough money and gumption to influence lawyers and judges to ensure his victory? Would Meg be yanked out from under him and forced into a marriage she doesn't want? What were the laws in Massachusetts about the rights of married women? Would she lose her inheritance to this guy if they wed?

He continued down the sidewalk. *Please God, work this out for Meg. Grant the agency your wisdom on who to contact and how to collect the information needed to set aside this lawsuit.* He arrived at the sheriff's office and put his hand on the knob. What if he offered to marry Meg? Would that solve her problem or make it worse?

Legacy of Love

Chapter Twenty-Four

Lightning flashed through the window as rain thrummed against the glass in sheets, blurring the trees outside. Seconds later, thunder cracked, and the house trembled. With a loud sigh Meg stuffed another skirt inside her satchel. The storm began shortly after she decided to leave Spruce Hill as if the heavens were weeping with her.

The only question remaining was whether she was packing for Boston or an unknown destination. Awake for most of the night, she'd tossed and turned then paced, yet hours later still hadn't made her choice. Visions of Tyler's leering face flitted through her mind, and she shuddered. Could she accept her fate and live with a man she neither loved nor trusted? Had God forsaken her to allow this to happen or was He punishing her? If she ran, would she be as Jonah? Heading for a terrible consequence until she gave herself up to God's will?

Too many unanswered questions. Tears slipped from her eyes, and she swiped at them. Crying was useless, yet she'd been unable to stem the flow. Could she be jailed for disobeying the summons and fleeing? She grimaced. Perhaps being sequestered in a cell was better than marriage to a cruel and heartless man.

She bit her lip and continued to toss clothing and personal effects into her bag. Not the Christmas morning she'd planned, but there was no reason to dally. She'd leave instructions for the rest of her things to be distributed to the needy. She hated to make others do her bidding, but she needed to get out of town without fanfare, especially since she wasn't going home with Reuben.

Reuben.

His eyes the color of the water in Boston Harbor on a summer day, crinkling at the corners when he laughed or smiled. Broad shoulders with muscles that rippled when he bent over the sink or lifted her into the wagon. Large hands that could heft the biggest loads or guide a small child's stick as he drew in the dirt. Then there was his kiss. Her toes curled at the remembrance of his lips on hers.

"Stop. Nothing can come of your feelings. Now, finish up and be on your way." Meg turned and caught sight of her reflection in the mirror above the dresser. Hair in disarray, she shook her head. Gray smudges darkened the skin below her eyes, and her cheeks were ashen. Lines crawled across her forehead. She'd seemed to age ten years since the receipt of yesterday's letter.

"It serves Tyler right to get an ugly wife." A harsh laugh bubbled up, then tears poured down her face, and she threw herself on the bed letting the sobs overtake her. *Why is this happening, God? Why would You make me marry a man I don't love and who doesn't love me. Or You. Please, save me.*

She stilled. Reuben had prayed with her about the situation yesterday, giving her a moment's peace that all would work out. But shortly after he'd left, she'd picked up her burden again, fretting and worrying through the rest of the day and night. Only now did she approach God, whom she claimed to love with all her heart, when she was desperate. What kind of believer was she?

One who didn't have the faith she claimed. *Forgive me, Lord. Whatever You would have me do. I'll not flee Your will as Jonah did.*

Warmth blanketed her as if a pair of strong arms wrapped themselves around her shoulders. The deluge outside lessened to a drizzle, and patches of blue appeared between the pewter-colored clouds. The tightness in her chest eased.

Banging sounded at her front door, and she pulled her pillow over her head. If she remained still, perhaps whoever it was would go away. The knocking continued, and a muffled voice shouted, "Meg. I've got news. Open the door."

"Reuben?"

So much for slipping out of town. *Not really, Lord.*

"Meg, I know you're in there. Please, open the door."

She rolled off the bed to her feet. "Just a minute." With swift strokes, she brushed her hair then plaited a single, long braid. She filled the ewer then dipped a cloth into the water and wiped her face. She dared not look in the mirror, or she'd change her mind about letting Reuben into the house.

"Coming. I'm coming." She smoothed her dress and straightened her spine. She licked her lips and twisted the knob. Reuben stood on the porch, hat in hand. Rain beaded on his suede coat. She stepped back and beckoned him inside.

His boots thudded on the floor as he walked past her then stopped in the center of the room. A smile hovered on his lips. "You may want to sit down."

Her heart pounded. "That bad?"

"No, that good."

She sank into the nearest chair, her hands plucking at her skirt. "Really?"

"I've already received a response to my telegram. Turns out the agency had begun investigating your...uh...our Mr. Armory. He should have kept a lower profile because he was seen by the brother of a woman he'd wronged."

"What? What woman?" Meg's hand flew to her throat.

"Sorry. I'll start at the beginning. Tyler Armory is an alias. His given name is Thomas Aitchison, and about ten years ago he married a rich widow, slowly cleaned out her accounts, then faked his death. He changed his name and showed up in Boston acting the part of a long-lost cousin to one of the city's oldest families. How he managed to get away with the act is beyond me. I would have thought they had the resources to ferret out his deception." He rubbed his jaw. "Anyway, his greed knows no bounds, so he set his sights on your family. Lots of money and a desire for respectability. Your parents played right into his hands, but then you up and ran out on them."

Her eyes widened as he talked. "Tyler's a fraud?"

"And a crook." He nodded. "The woman's brother reported the sighting and the history of what he'd done to his sister to the police and Armory...er...Aitchison's been arrested. Needless to say, the suit against you is invalid."

Meg slumped in the chair and pressed her hand to her mouth. Traitorous tears seeped from her eyes. This time from relief.

Reuben fumbled for a handkerchief and knelt in front of her, dabbing at the wetness on her cheeks. "God has allowed the man's thievery to come to light. Everything has worked out." His smile was hesitant. "Listen, I'm sorry for pushing you to return to Boston with me. I was wrong. The decision is completely yours to make, and I was out of line making you prove yourself to me. I am merely an agent, and I took it upon myself to insert myself into your business. Please forgive me."

"You've been a good friend. I know that in your heart you felt my accepting Aunt Ida's estate could change my life for the better." She squeezed his shoulder. "There's no need to apologize."

He grabbed her hand and kissed her palm then pressed her hand to his chest. His heart thumped steadily beneath her fingers as his gaze caressed her face. "I hope I've become more than a friend, Meg. You've burrowed your way inside me as I never thought any woman could ever do. I didn't want to say anything, but I can no longer keep my feelings hidden."

Her breath caught. He cared for her? He had been telling the truth when he spoke to the pastor. She wasn't imagining the bond that connected them.?

"Please tell me you feel the same way. That I hold a special place in your heart." He stroked the back of her hand with his thumb.

Shivering at his touch, she whispered, "As no man has ever done."

A smile bloomed on his face, and he pulled her into his arms, encircling her in a tight embrace.

She sighed. Whether she was in Oregon or Boston or somewhere in between, as long as she was beside Reuben, she was home.

Epilogue

The sea of smiling faces shimmered as Meg's eyes filled with tears. Everyone she knew, and then some, had crowded into the café for her wedding. She and Reuben had spent the rest of Christmas day reveling in each other's company and making plans for the future. Their future. After much conversation and prayer, they'd decided to get married the morning of New Year's Eve and catch the afternoon train to Boston.

She'd notified Amy of their engagement the next day, and her friend had single-handedly arranged the entire event. She'd even taken Meg shopping for a new dress. All in less than a week. Just in time for her and Reuben to begin 1872 as man and wife.

The ceremony was over, and the reception breakfast was in full swing. Laughter and conversation mingled with the sound of silverware on china, footsteps on the wooden floors, and guitar music.

Her groom stood across the room talking with Sheriff Hobbs and his son, Tad. Reuben must have felt her gaze, because he turned and sent her a dazzling smile, his eyes gleaming. Her stomach fluttered, and her pulse raced. How was it possible that this handsome, kind, and generous man had chosen her?

"How are you holding up?" Amy appeared at her elbow, a mug of coffee in her hand. "You look beautiful."

"Thanks." Meg blew out a deep breath. "Exhausted, but in a good way, you know?"

"I do." She gave Meg a one-armed hug. "I'm so happy for you. Reuben seems like a great guy, and he's totally smitten with you."

"The feeling is mutual." She glanced at him again, noting his wide shoulders and the lock of hair that had fallen over his forehead.

"With all the preparations we didn't get a chance to talk much about what you two decided to do other than go East. Will you stay in your aunt's house?"

Meg shook her head. "I've been waiting for a telegram before sharing the news. We'll sell the house and most of its contents, only bringing those pieces with sentimental value. I'm going to use some of the money to purchase the café. I received Mrs. Krause's response last night. She wants to retire and be near her daughter, so this is perfect timing."

Amy gave her another hug and squealed. "That's wonderful. You'll be staying in town. I was so afraid you'd stay in Boston."

"Not a chance. We'll be there a while, perhaps as much as six months because of taking care of the estate, but I'll also be spending time with my family." Tears pricked the backs of her eyes. She'd cried more in the last week than she'd ever done, but mostly tears of joy. "I've heard back from them, too, and they can't wait to see me. We have a lot of lost time to make up for." She tucked a stray hair behind her ear. "We'll also be using some of the funds to support the orphanage, but the best part is that we're probably going to be adopting Lem."

"That's fantastic. I know he's meant a lot to you."

"Yes, he's a child of my heart. Nothing's set in stone, but we've met with the Quinns and begun the process. We won't say anything to Lem until after we get back." Meg's lip trembled. "Wouldn't be fair to raise his hopes in case the adoption doesn't work out or someone else decides to take him."

"I don't believe that will happen." Amy grinned. "Life sure has turned upside down for you in a short time, but what a blessed way to start 1872. A new husband, a new business, and a child. Wonder what else is in store for you?"

The door swung open, and the young man who was watching the general store for Mr. Densley entered the café gripping a tiny envelope. Meg's heart pounded. Were telegrams going to be the bane of her existence? His gaze swept the room before coming to rest on Reuben. Wending his way through the crowd, the clerk handed over the cable with a nod.

"I'm about to find out, Amy." She lifted her skirts and rushed across the room, her eyes riveted on her new husband, whose passive expression belied any tension he might be feeling. She arrived at his side and sent a distracted smile at the sheriff.

"I'll leave you to it, Reuben. Good luck." Sheriff Hobbs patted Meg's shoulder before sauntering away, his son on his heels.

"What is it? Were you expecting a cable? You don't look surprised."

"Relax." He pressed a gentle kiss on her lips. "I'm sure it's a congratulatory message from Mr. Pinkerton. I haven't heard from him since wiring him the news of our marriage and your decision about the bequest."

"Oh, of course." The tightness in her chest eased. "I'm a bit skittish about telegrams."

He chuckled. "I understand." He slid a finger under the flap then pulled out the small sheet of paper. As he scanned the document, his eyebrow shot up. "As I suspected and more. Listen: 'Sending my deepest felicitations to you and Miss Underwood. Wishing you speedy and safe travel to Boston. Will meet you there in the near future to discuss your appointment as director of the Northwest region.' For a frugal Scotsman, he sure used a lot of words."

Snatching the paper, she stared at the words. "A promotion. You're getting a promotion."

"Yes, but perhaps I prefer to remain as the café's dishwasher."

"Ha. How do you know the job is still yours?"

He snaked his arm around her waist and tugged her toward him, his eyes snapping with delight. "Because I'm acquainted with the prospective owner, and I believe I may have some clout."

Meg twisted her mouth in a mock pout and pressed her hands against his chest. "Just a little."

"Then I'll have to work on increasing my influence." He bent his head and kissed her, gently at first, then with more insistence, his lips warm and full of promise.

She giggled and melted into his embrace. "I look forward to negotiations."

"As do I."

THE END

Legacy of Love

What did you think of *Legacy of Love?*

Thank you so much for purchasing *Legacy of Love*. You could have selected any number of books to read, but you chose this book.

I hope it added encouragement and exhortation to your life. If so, it would be nice if you could share this book with your family and friends by posting to Facebook (www.facebook.com) and/or Twitter (www.twitter.com).

If you enjoyed this book and found some benefit in reading it, I'd appreciate it if you could take some time to post a review on Amazon, Goodreads, Kobo, GooglePlay, Apple Books, or other book review site of your choice. Your feedback and support will help me to improve my writing craft for future projects and make this book even better.
Thank you again for your purchase.

Blessings,
Linda Shenton Matchett

Acknowledgments

Although writing a book is a solitary task, it is not a solitary journey. There have been many who have helped and encouraged me along the way.

My parents, Richard and Jean Shenton, who presented me with my first writing tablet and encouraged me to capture my imagination with words. Thanks, Mom and Dad!

Scribes212 – my ACFW online critique group: Valerie Goree, Marcia Lahti, and the late Loretta Boyett (passed on to Glory, but never forgotten). Without your input, my writing would not be nearly as effective.

Eva Marie Everson – my mentor/instructor with Christian Writers' Guild. You took a timid, untrained student and turned her into a writer. Many thanks!

SincNE, and the folks who coordinate the Crimebake Writing Conference. I have attended many writing conferences, but without a doubt, Crimebake is one of the best. The workshops, seminars, panels, critiques, and every tiny aspect are well-executed, professional, and educational.

Special thanks to Hank Phillippi Ryan, Halle Ephron, and Roberta Isleib for your encouragement and spot-on critiques of my work.

Thanks to my Book Brigade who provide information, encouragement, and support.

Paula Proofreader (https://paulaproofreader.wixsite.com/home): I'm so glad I found you! My work is cleaner because of your eagle eye. Any mistakes are completely mine.

A heartfelt thank you to my brothers, Jack Shenton and Douglas Shenton, and my sister, Susan Shenton Greger for being enthusiastic cheerleaders during my writing journey. Your support means more than you'll know.

My husband, Wes, deserves special kudos for understanding my need to write. Thank you for creating my writing room – it's perfect, and I'm thankful for it every day. Thank you for your willingness to accept a house that's a bit cluttered, laundry that's not always done, and meals on the go. I love you.

And finally, to God be the glory. I thank Him for giving me the gift of writing and the inspiration to tell stories that shine the light on His goodness and mercy.

Want more romance? Read on for the first chapter of *Spies &*
Sweethearts, Sisters in Service, book 1.

Chapter One

Just because she was the eldest, did Cora have to criticize Emily's every decision? She was a high school French teacher, not a schoolgirl. Shaking her head, Emily climbed on the bike and pedaled away from the house. She'd exhausted her gas rations for the week, so using the car was out. Fortunately, the library wasn't far. She could finish preparing the end-of-year exams there.

Two of her students were already gone. Days after they turned eighteen, the boys talked the principal into letting them graduate early in order to enlist. Her heart constricted. Now, both were in training with the army air force and would soon be on their way overseas to fight the Germans. They spoke French impeccably, a skill better used in the ambassador ranks rather than on an airplane.

The warm air stroked Emily's cheeks as she rode. Squinting against the sun's glare, she huffed out a breath. At least the boys were doing something for the war effort. Her service with the American Women's Voluntary Services as a plane spotter and messenger wasn't exactly going to turn the tide against the Axis powers. Surely, there was something more she could do.

She braked in front of the sandstone building and wheeled her bike into an empty spot in one of the racks near the entrance of Trafalgar Public Library. A Carnegie library, it housed several hundred books thanks to the Scottish-American philanthropist. What would he think of the war?

"Emily!"

A broad grin on her face, Joan Boyer hurried toward Emily. Her floral dress danced around her leg, and her ponytail flounced. "Your mom said I'd find you here." Her smile faltered. "Are you okay? You look terrible."

"Gee, thanks. Glad I can count on you for support."

"What?"

Emily finger-combed her hair. "I'm sorry. I had another argument with Cora. Just because she's already been married and widowed, she thinks she knows what's good for everyone."

Joan linked her arm through Emily's. "Let's grab a seat in the memorial garden. You can tell me everything."

They sauntered to the wooden bench sheltered by a large, weeping cherry tree and surrounded by black-eyed Susans, and a rainbow of coneflowers and petunias nodding in the breeze.

"All right. What gives? You've been annoyed with Cora in the past, but you seem especially angry today."

"I am." Emily slumped against the seat. "True or not, it feels like neither she nor Doris take me seriously because I'm the youngest. That all I'm good enough for is teaching a bunch of kids. A few days ago, Cora commented that plane spotting night duty must be interfering with my job, and she didn't understand why I was still volunteering. Like I can't juggle multiple responsibilities. I'm almost twenty-six years old. I'm quite capable."

"Maybe she worries about you."

"Perhaps, but it doesn't seem like concern. It feels like criticism of my life." Emily fisted her hands. "This morning, I got a letter telling me I've been accepted into a new government program. I leave for training the day after school is out. She overheard me telling Mom about the job and quizzed me about it. When I told her I couldn't share specifics, she rolled her eyes and asked what the government needed with a schoolteacher."

"That's awful." Joan squeezed Emily's shoulder.

"The worst of it is that once she got started down that road, Mom followed…said I should rethink the opportunity…that I have a perfectly good job here at home, and my volunteer work is sufficient." She frowned. "Then Mom said I'm being selfish to go off on my own. It's bad enough I'm still living at home at my age, but for them to try to dictate my decisions is too much."

"What are you going to do?"

"Send a telegram accepting the position. I've got to live my own life no matter what they say." She blinked away tears forming in her eyes. "Do you think I'm being self-centered by going?"

"Absolutely not. Your parents are in perfect health, and Cora is living here, too. She can take care of any needs they might have." Joan leaned forward. "You really can't say much about the job? Not even a little?"

The tightness in Emily's chest eased, and she chuckled. "You always could make me feel better. I'm sorry for not telling you I applied, but I was skeptical I'd get selected. You should have seen the crowd. Anyway, I don't know a lot about the job. There is a new governmental department, and it needs people who are bilingual. The exam contained lots of translation exercises, especially with regard to colloquialisms and dialect for different regions in France and French-speaking countries."

"Now you know how your students feel."

"Absolutely, but that doesn't mean I'm going to go easy on them for the final." Emily rubbed her damp palms on her skirt. "I can't believe this will be my last year of teaching for a while…maybe forever. I'm a bit nervous about notifying the principal about leaving. The factories pay much higher than the schools, so Medford has had a lot of resignations. The school may have to combine classes next year."

"This war won't last forever. In fact, some say it will be over by Christmas. Surely you'll be back."

Emily shook her head. "I don't want to be a naysayer, but I doubt the war will be over by the end of the year. I think we're in this for the long haul."

"Can you at least tell me where you're going? I could come visit."

"I've forgotten the address, somewhere in Washington, DC, but that's not my final stop. I'll be transported with other new employees to the training facility where I'll stay for three months. I won't be able to send or receive letters while I'm there. And definitely no visitors."

Joan bolted upright. "That sounds intriguing, very secretive. If you're lucky, there will be a few dreamboats in the class."

"Romance is the last thing I need, Joan. Besides, guys our age are in the defense industry or armed forces. There won't be anyone to fall in love with."

Gerard Lucas resisted the urge to run a finger around the collar of his dress uniform to loosen the stifling piece of clothing. What he wouldn't give to be in a flannel shirt and pair of overalls. Out in the field, wind ruffling his hair, and acres of crops flourishing in the sunshine. Perhaps a beautiful woman by his side. And—

"Lieutenant Lucas, are you listening to me?"

Gerard wrenched his thoughts back to the present and snapped his heels together. "Sir, yes, sir."

"Insulting and then arguing with a higher ranking officer in front of his men and the local Brits is a serious offense. The only things keeping you out of the brig or a dishonorable discharge are this war and the fact you didn't take a poke at him. The country needs all the men we can get." Major Albert shook his head. "You're a bright guy, one who should be climbing the ranks rather than getting demoted every three months. You are lucky Major Quigley had you reduced to private."

"Sir, he didn't know what he was talking about—"

"I did not give you permission to speak, and therein lies your problem. Failure to respect the chain of command. You are to obey orders without question and to show respect to those ranked above you. You're arrogant and argumentative. More than a few officers have made that observation. Not a good combination, Lucas." The major dropped into the chair behind his desk. "You need to apologize to Major Quigley. In public. At the pub where the incident occurred."

"Yes, sir."

"Excellent. Now, the good news for everyone is that you are being transferred to an intelligence unit based out of Washington, DC. Apparently, your penchant for getting into trouble is a desirable trait to them."

Gerard's heart sped up. There'd been stories about guerrilla warfare and espionage, but he figured the information was rumor, like most of what he heard in between training exercises. Was he finally going to see the war up close? Or rather, behind the scenes?

Major Albert tossed him a set of papers then gestured to the vacant chair. "At ease, Soldier."

Dropping into the seat, Gerard tugged at his collar and sighed. The material still scratched his skin and threatened to suffocate him. He picked his orders and scanned the instructions. He had two days to prepare. To wait and wonder what was in store for him.

"As you can see, you leave the day after tomorrow. Unless you run into a hitch, you'll report for duty on Saturday. Try not to mess this up. It may be your last chance to remain a free man."

"Permission to speak candidly, sir?"

"I'd expect nothing less, Lucas."

"Why me?"

"Why you, what?"

"You must have recommended me, sir. Otherwise, how would they know about me?" Gerard studied the major. "So why did you put my name forward for consideration?"

"It appears I haven't underestimated your abilities. You're right. I did recommend you." Major Albert smirked. "This new department…they're calling it the Office of Strategic Services…a positively bureaucratic label, if you ask me, but maybe that's what they want everyone to think. Personally, from the bits and pieces I've been able to glean, it's more like the department of dirty tricks. Anyway, that sounded like something you'd be suited for. You know, swimming against the tide."

"I appreciate your faith in me, sir. I won't let you down."

"It's not me I'm worried about. Don't let yourself down, Lucas. You've got to come to terms with whatever's eating you. Yes, you don't suffer fools, and that's fine, but it's more than that. You're carting around a lot of anger. Maybe you know why. Maybe you don't. Either way, you need to channel those feelings or jettison them, because if you don't, you'll get yourself killed. Understood?"

"Yes, sir."

Major Albert steepled his fingers. "Quigley wanted to bring you up on charges, put you through a court-martial, but I talked him out of it."

"Thank you, sir."

"I'm not looking for gratitude. I'm telling you because this is your last chance. Not everyone is willing to accept your shenanigans. And despite the roguish nature of your new assignment, there will be some sort of hierarchy. Adhere to it, or you may not survive this war." He rose and extended his hand. "Good luck, son, and Godspeed."

They shook hands. Gerard put on his peaked wool cap, saluted, then pivoted and hurried from the room, a grin tugging at his lips. Finally, a chance to avenge his brother's death in the Atlantic at the hands of a German submarine wolfpack.

Other Titles
Romance

Love's Harvest, Wartime Brides, Book 1

Love's Rescue, Wartime Brides, Book 2

Love's Belief, Wartime Brides, Book 3

Love's Allegiance, Wartime Brides, Book 4

Love Found in Sherwood Forest

A Love Not Forgotten

On the Rails

A Doctor in the House

Spies & Sweethearts, Sisters in Service, Book 1

The Mechanic & the MD, Sisters in Service, Book 2

The Widow & the War Correspondent, Sisters in Service, Book 3

Dinah's Dilemma (Westward Home & Hearts Mail-Order Brides, 10)

Love at First Flight

A Bride for Seamus (Proxy Bride series, 54)

Mystery

Under Fire, Ruth Brown Mystery Series, Book 1

Under Ground, Ruth Brown Mystery Series, Book 2

Under Cover, Ruth Brown Mystery Series, Book 3

Murder of Convenience, Women of Courage, Book 1

Murder at Madison Square Garden, Women of Courage, Book 2

Non-Fiction

WWII Word Find, Volume 1

Biography

Linda Shenton Matchett writes about ordinary people who did extraordinary things in days gone by. She is a volunteer docent and archivist at the Wright Museum of WWII and a trustee for her local public library. Born in Baltimore, Maryland, a stone's throw from Fort McHenry, she has lived in historical places most of her life. Now located in central New Hampshire, Linda's favorite activities include exploring historic sites and immersing herself in the imaginary worlds created by other authors.

Website/blog: http://www.LindaShentonMatchett.com
Facebook: http://www.facebook.com/LindaShentonMatchettAuthor
Pinterest: http://www.pinterest.com/lindasmatchett
Amazon: https://www.amazon.com/Linda-Shenton-Matchett/e/B01DNB54S0
Goodreads: http://www.goodreads.com/author_linda_matchett
Bookbub: http://www.bookbub.com/authors/linda-shenton-matchett

tained

243